THE HEALING BLADE

ALSO BY ALEXANDER CORDELL

The White Cockade
Witches' Sabbath

THE
HEALING BLADE

Alexander Cordell

THE VIKING PRESS   NEW YORK

For Maurice James Elliott,
age thirteen,
of County Tyrone

Contents

In life, the blade that severs;
in death, the blade that heals.

Anonymous

A Light on the Shore

"Light on the larboard bow!" wailed the helmsman.

Thunder crashed and reverberated over the black wastes of the sea. The little fishing smack put her nose down into the rollers and rose high, spraying foam, and her scuppers ran full, hissing above the roar of the channel tide.

"There it is again!" cried Patrick, pointing, and we gripped the heaving rail and wiped spray from our faces. Distantly, flickering through the mist, a lantern waved on the rocky headland of Pas-de-Calais. Above the treble howl of the wind I heard the agonized creaking of the blocks; the sails flapped and beat like drums above the rushing sea. Glancing aloft, I saw lightning fork in jagged flashes across a watery dawn.

"Light on the larboard bow, I say!" shouted the helmsman astern, and he fought the wheel, his squat body leaping against the sky.

Marcel Robet, the skipper, came on deck then. "I hear helmsman call?" he asked. Patrick gripped his arm, pointing, and shouted above the wind, "Look—two points larboard—the lantern!"

"Aha! Very good navigation, eh? Where would you Irish patriots be without French sailors?" Turning, he shouted into my face, "When Bonaparte burns the town of Bristol, it will be because of us, you agree?"

"Better take us in," said Patrick.

"I not take orders from you—I take orders from the master. *Voilà!*" He spat at our feet and grinned happily.

"Is this the rendezvous, Robet?" I demanded.

"It is the rendezvous, Monsieur, as I promised. The place, the time are as I said. Now it is up to you. I return to Ireland, and you go on to hell. *Mes enfants!* I pity you in the chambers of the French counterspies."

I glanced at Patrick. No emotion was in his face, this my companion in this fateful mission for the honor of Ireland. To Patrick Hays, strong, mature, one mission was like another. The fact that we might end up on an oar in the whiplashed galleys of Spain, or rot in some French dungeon did not seem to occur to him. I was seventeen years old, Patrick was nearer twenty-seven. And in the ten years between us he had packed more danger and excitement as a spy for our country than most men did in their whole lives.

Marcel Robet said, at the companionway door, "You have heard of the Black Midget?"

Patrick gripped the rail at a sudden buck of the deck. "We have, Robet."

"And you will not forget him, I vow. More than one Irishman he has sent to the galleys. You turn your back on

Petit Pierre, the midget, and *whoof!*" Robet drew his finger across his throat. "He will cut it deep from ear to ear."

"I'll look forward to that," said Patrick. "Now get below to Caine Adams, man. You are wasting your time up here, for you are frightening nobody but yourself."

"One day, Irishman, you will laugh on the other side of your face. When Petit Pierre is done with you, he will sell you to the galleys of Spain."

I shrugged, turning away, and the Frenchman winked at me as he went. He was a strange concoction of loyalty and hate, this one, and I envied the way Patrick handled him. I also envied my friend's courage.

Death, my father had taught me, is acceptable when one is in the service of a country as beloved as Ireland, and the manner of death usually cost me no sleep. Yet, strangely, the thought of ending my days in the galleys never failed to terrify me. Once, when my father was alive, he brought home a friend to Milford in Wales. This man, in his twenty-fourth year, had spent six of them aboard the Spanish galleys. Enfeebled, tottering on the edge of the grave, he was a man broken; a blinded wretch, his body mutilated by the whip, his wrists and ankles cankered by the overseer's chains.

Patrick grinned at me. "They have to catch ye first, son," he said. "Come, get below. I can hear the old man calling."

I glanced shoreward as I followed Patrick down to the

little cabin where Caine Adams, the Irish patriot, was waiting to brief us. I saw the lantern again, withering and dancing, a weird, unearthly sign.

I shivered.

For God, for Honor, for Ireland

Caine Adams sat motionless at the table, his eyes opaque in their blindness. He had given his soul to Ireland in her fight for freedom; his eyes he had given to the dreaded Hompesch, the German mercenary regiment brought in by the British to help suppress our rebellion.

Caine Adams said then, "Are ye listening, John Regan? For though I can hear Pat Hays' breathing, there's not a sound of yours."

"I am here, sir." I answered and squared my feet to the rolling deck.

"And is the cabin door shut fast, men, for I don't care for the smell o' that Frenchman Robet."

"Give me five minutes with him before we leave, sir," said Patrick.

"None o' that! He's warranted by the highest in the French Directory and they reckon, for all his cheek, he's a fine patriot man. Save your energy for the midget, for you'll need it."

"Yet ye don't trust him yourself, sir?" I asked.

"I have no option, for he's a fine navigator. Is it right the light's bright off St-Valery?"

"Like a shooting star," said Patrick.

"Right," said the blind man. "Then we'll get the hang o' the plan once more, for I'm not repeating it again. Come closer."

Like some ancient patriarch he looked, sitting there, the shadows flung by the lamp deep in his wrinkled face, for his youth had been lost in his scheming and suffering for an independent Ireland. His snow-white hair dropped in gentle waves to his shoulders. I held the hilt of my rapier tight, staring down at him.

"Place your right hands on the table before me," he said, and we obeyed and he gripped our wrists with astonishing strength, saying, "Let me drive a beloved name through your veins, you two, for you'll be carrying in these hands the life of the greatest Irishman of the age."

"Wolfe Tone," I said. This much we already knew.

"Aye, the great man himself. And ye're privileged indeed that the Rebel Committee should honor your name with the duty. This is the saviour we have prayed for since 1791. Bring him safely to Ireland's shores and you'll be entered on the scroll of Ireland's glory. Fail her, and your children's children will be cursed for a thousand years from Cork to Londonderry by decent Irish people. Are ye listening?"

"Yes, sir," I replied.

The sea took the little smack and heeled her then, hitting her brutally along her shanks, and she shrieked high in pain, like a stallion under the whip. The rollers thundered beyond the cabin, and the wind howled at us in fury.

Caine Adams said, "On the face of it, our rebellion against the rule of England is defeated. Our motherland is abandoned to the brutal English soldiery. Our rebel leaders, from Bagenal Harvey of Wexford to the wonderful Father John Murphy, have died the deaths of felons on the scaffolds o' the English conquerors. Our country blazes from Antrim to Cork; the bayonets of a foreign infantry are driving our women and children into the bogs and fastnesses, as they were driven into barren Connaught two hundred years ago by the sword of the beast Cromwell." He raised his haggard face to the ceiling. "Dear God, have pity on this unhappy land! Put an end to the tortures and the transportations. Oh, God, take pity!" Still gripping our wrists, he lowered his head, whispering, "For never, even under Robespierre in France, has there been such a terror. Never did a government of civilized men pursue extermination with so bloody a hand!"

Stilled by his passion, I stood white-faced before him.

For our rebellion against England had been crushed, and the red-breasted dragoons of England were taking revenge for the uprising. Under the terrible British General Lake and puppets like Lord Kingsborough, my people were being quelled. Sixty and more of our most prominent rebel leaders had been hanged on Wexford Bridge and their heads paraded around the town on pikes. And with these, the new heroes of my generation, were now dying thousands of their followers, from patriotic priests like Father Roche and Father Sweeney to innocent peasants and merchants of the cities. And at the head of the atrocities against the helpless stood the turncoat Irish yeomen and militia, who were licking the heels of England for favor, and the terrible Hompesch, who killed for a pastime.

Now Caine Adams cried, "But although the Wexford rebellion has been crushed, we will rise again. We will rise again under the leadership of the greatest patriot of all—Theobald Wolfe Tone. And with the help of our French allies, he will invade the shores of Ireland and bring peace to our beloved land. *Wolfe Tone!*" The old man rose feebly, tears on his face.

"May God bless and preserve the beloved name, sir," said Patrick softly.

"Then let us to it," whispered Caine Adams, gripping the bulkhead against the rush and pitch of the cabin, "for enough today of idle, impassioned speeches. They brook no action; they're but a heap o' wasted breath, and it's breath you'll need, Patrick Hays and John Regan, to obey all that Ireland orders. *Listen again.* It is the intention of Wolfe Tone to bring an army of Bonaparte's Frenchmen to our shores, and drive the invading British into the sea. But his enemies are all about him; the spies of England hear his every footfall; the weapons of England and a cursed Irish gentry threaten him on every side. Repeat your task, John Regan!"

His sightless eyes turned to me. I said, "The task is to protect the life of our leader, Wolfe Tone, and to die for this if need be."

"Right, you!" He turned to Patrick. "Relate the method, and drive it into your brains."

Patrick took a deep breath and said, "We are to enter the spy ring of the English and learn their intentions. We are to execute any man who threatens the life of Tone; we are to afford him safe journeys in his comings and goings. We will accompany his French expedition when it sails for the shores of Ireland."

"Excellent," whispered the blind man. "Now name the date, time, and place of the proposed landing by Wolfe Tone on Irish soil, Regan."

I answered softly, "On the twenty-eighth day of this month of September, at dawn, the French invasion force will land at Kinvarra in Galway Bay."

"Correct. Patrick Hays—name the numbers in the invasion force, the senior naval officer commanding it, and the place in France from which it will set sail."

Patrick replied, "The number of Frenchmen sailing will be nearly thirty thousand. The force will be commanded by Commodore Rochelle of Nevin. There will be three ships of the line and fifty frigates: Wolfe Tone will be aboard the *Expedite*. The expedition will set sail from Cherbourg. The French troops are already stationed at barracks in Tourlaville, on that peninsula."

"Excellent," said Adams. "The Rebel Committee has

briefed you well. It is necessary to our plan that you should both possess such vital information, but I hope you realize the dangers of having it?"

We nodded, muttering assent, and he added, "Then be aware of this, too. You carry in your heads enough planning to destroy Wolfe Tone's expedition before it leaves port. And he has been scheming and quarreling with his French allies these past four years for a decent assault against the English in our country." He made a fist of his hand. "So, in the face of the whip, the screw, the branding iron—not a word—on your holy honor!"

"I give my word on it," said I.

"And I give mine," said Patrick Hays.

Caine Adams drew forth a Bible, saying, "Place your right hands on this. Now swear by God that not a breath of the committee's instructions shall pass your lips, even though your bodies be given to the flames."

Facing him, we gave this pledge, and he said, "Right then, the immediate plan of action. Begin it, John Regan."

I replied, "A few minutes from now we swim ashore, following the light on the headland . . ."

"Who is signaling with the lantern?"

"An Irish patriot of these parts, but he has no name. Robet knows him."

"Aye. And then?"

I said, "Two miles down the road to Abbeville we will ambush the coach of Monsieur Jean Le Garde, a traitor to the new republic, and his friend Captain Paul Wentworth, an English spy sent in from London . . ."

"Paul Wentworth, the man sent to assassinate Wolfe Tone, remember!"

"Aye." I continued. "Patrick takes Le Garde's clothes. I take the clothes of Captain Wentworth. We impersonate these men, being of their size and akin to them in looks— this is why we were chosen ..."

"You are doing well. Proceed," said Caine Adams.

"The Irish patriot who beckoned with the lantern will take the clothes of the coachman—"

"And then?" Adams turned to Patrick Hays, and Patrick replied, "The coach horses will be set free. Our own horses will be set in the shafts. The patriot will drive us in the coach to a hamlet outside Beauvais, where we will stay for the night at an inn called the Creton Belle. There, a man with a shattered face—"

"Enough of detail," said the old man. "What happens when you reach Paris?" He turned to me.

I said, "At Chantilly, outside Paris, we abandon the coach. The Irish patriot returns to his village on this coast. Mounting our own horses, we ride to the Bastille area."

"To what address?"

Patrick said, "Cellar number sixteen, Rue de Victoire, sir. We report there to Monsieur Petit Pierre, head of the English spy agency in Paris. We inform him that we, Monsieur Jean Le Garde and Captain Paul Wentworth, have arrived from Calais to be in his service."

"Correct. And after that?"

"After that it is the will of God," I said.

There was a moment of silence—even the sea seemed to

be listening. Then the storm beat about us with a new fury. The little boat lurched and shuddered in a flurry of wind; wet fingers streamed down the cabin window; the lantern of the headland faintly gleamed on the glass.

Caine Adams said, "You have been well briefed. But you realize the extent of the danger in impersonating this Frenchman and British officer? I say again—you realize what will happen if you are unmasked and fall into the hands of Petit Pierre, the Black Midget?"

"Yes, sir," we said, and the old man added, "Nevertheless, I am instructed by the committee to warn you once more of the extent of the danger. That even if you succeed in bringing Wolfe Tone safely to the point of departure in France, the effort may cost you your lives. The midget is no fool. I am to tell you that Petit Pierre is in touch with the recruiter of the Spanish Admirality." He turned away his face. "A stream of our best agents have ended their lives amid the terrors of the Spanish galleys. You know what this means?"

Patrick grinned happily. As for me, the sweat sprang to my face and ran in a hot trickle down the nape of my neck. As if recognizing the sudden terror in me, Caine Adams turned his sightless eyes toward my face.

"You do understand what it means, John Regan?"

"If I'm rowing for anyone, I'm doin' it for Ireland, sir," I said.

"You are brave men. God grant ye peace, my friends. Now, call the skipper, Marcel Robet."

A strange thing happened then. As Patrick opened the

cabin door to call him, Marcel Robet entered with a bow, and Patrick flashed a glance at me.

"I am here, Monsieur Adams. I expected you to call me." He stood to attention before the table.

"Your position, man?"

"Half a mile off the headland. I am now sailing in, as instructed."

"It is safe water? The horses have to swim."

"They could swim ten miles in this water—in the shelter of the headland, Pas-de-Calais is like a pond."

"And the weather?"

"The weather is moderating, Monsieur."

"Then take us in. How close can you get with safety?"

"Two hundred yards—it is less than nothing."

Caine Adams raised his face slowly to the Frenchman. "I pray you are right. The currents can be dangerous along Pas-de-Calais, I am told."

"Not off St-Valery, Monsieur." Marcel Robet beamed assurance.

"Especially off St-Valery."

The Frenchman shrugged. "French horses, French spies —for these it would be easy." He grinned amiably. "But I cannot speak for Irish ones."

"Enough," said Caine Adams. "Dismiss and prepare."

And Patrick said to Robet as he closed the cabin door behind him, "Ye know something, Robet—I canna think why Caine Adams trusts you."

"But why not?" The Frenchman spread his hands. "Am I not a fighter for the new French *republique?* Was I not three times wounded in the service of my beloved Napoleon? I fight for France and Ireland, Monsieur, the same as you!"

"Sometimes it doesn't sound like it," said Patrick.

"And I risk my life to bring you safely to St-Valery?"

I turned away. Nerves were taut, tempers at the breaking point, and knives were in the air. Right from the start of this expedition Patrick had not trusted Marcel Robet.

"Och, he's all right," I said, after he had gone. "He's just boisterous."

"I don't trust him, and I can't think why."

"If Caine Adams does, it's all right by me," I said.

The door opened behind us. "Are ye there, Hays?" called Adams from the cabin.

"Aye, here, sir," replied Patrick.

Frail as a starved ghost the old man looked in the doorway, and his voice was but a whisper. He said, "One last thing, and this is for nobody's ears but the two of yours. If you're on the run after you get Wolfe Tone on the soil of Ireland, there's a friend who'll serve ye well in Dublin. And if ever ye land in the barracks of Dublin, ye can put your lives in the hands of this one—Derry O'Shea, of the inn called the English Trader. Can ye remember that?"

"Derry O'Shea," I repeated, "of the English Trader."

"He's the best agent in Ireland for getting men out o' the gates of hell," said Caine Adams. "Now away, an' good luck to ye."

A Soldier of Fortune

Marcel Robet, for all his arrogance, was a fine skipper. He took his little craft to within two hundred yards of the French coast before pulling over the helm to tack in gusty sweeps across the still water seaward of the breakers. The big brown stallion shied, I noticed, fearing the plunge, but my beloved Mia flattened her ears and snorted, loving it, and as Robet parted the rail she leaped, kicking strongly. Both she and Patrick's horse had been trained for this, and I wondered at the stallion's reluctance. With Mia swimming powerfully beneath me, I glanced over my shoulder and saw Patrick bringing up the horse's head and clamping him hard with his knees. Only when Robet struck his hindquarter did he leap, doing so with a scream of fear. Now he was in, plunging madly, while Patrick fought for balance.

There exists, deep in the mind of a horse, a knowledge of the unknown. My father used to say, "Beware when a good horse cries with fear."

Now the breakers were coming up before us, hissing in

wild-flung crests before their pounding run for the beach. And Mia split them, tossing back her wet mane into my face, and stretched her great forelegs, keeping me high.

"Up, girl, up!" I cried to her, and instantly we were into the foaming maelstrom of the crested rollers, delighting in the thunder of it. The sea lifted us high with maniacal strength and carried us forward, now tugging us back into the hollow, swirling troughs, to flounder madly until the next breaker in caught us in its arms, flinging us on. Often, on Pembroke sands in Wales, Mia and I had played this game, which my father had taught us. And as her flailing hoofs cut sand she rose, streaming, and I glanced over my shoulder to see how Patrick and the stallion were faring.

The sea was empty.

I saw the cutthroat sail of Marcel Robet's boat tacking swiftly across the bay, but of Patrick there was no sign. Wading into the sea, I dived under the first breaker and struck out strongly for the comparatively slack water beyond. Panic was growing in me as I reached it, and I rose in the sea, gasping and flinging water from my hair.

"Patrick, Patrick!"

With all my strength I impelled my body onward, searching the dim wastes under that cold, September dawn. Nothing moved on the sea—only the receding sail of the fishing smack, now a lonely dot beyond the bay. And then it happened. A sudden thrust of underwater current took my legs from beneath me as I trod water, upending me, and an icy hand of astonishing power gripped me. In a surging tide the sea cascaded about my waist and legs. It rushed in a black flood, first tossing me up, then dragging me down. The rushing darkness of the sea beat in my ears as I clawed my way to the surface, fighting for breath. Then I was sucked down again and volleyed along the sand of the channel like a scrap of paper borne on the wind. And as my heart began to pulsate in my ears, I was thrown up into warmer water. The tide passed in sucks and whirlpools, and the incoming breakers took me again. Then, as if tired of drowning people, the sea relented. Helpless on her breast, she carried me in and flung me high into the shallows where Mia was standing. Arms and legs outstretched I lay, then knelt, retching. And Mia stared down at me, as if perplexed by the astonishing behavior of humans. For she had brought me out of the sea only to watch me dive back into it.

Later, when my strength returned, I found Patrick. He was lying in the shallows half a mile down the beach. His hair, I remember, was streaming over his face.

With Mia watching over us, I squatted in the sand and gathered my friend in my arms. A little wind, as if in solace, whimpered over the beach.

I wept.

Later still, I rose, knowing a great and fearful emptiness. Patrick Hays, upon whose strength and authority the success of this mission mainly depended, was dead. Caine

Adams, who commanded it, was beyond the horizon. I looked at the sun. It was nearly seven o'clock. The Irish patriot who had beckoned with the lantern would be waiting at the crossroads two miles from St-Valery down the road to Abbeville, and I was already late for the rendezvous. Rising, I gazed down at Patrick's face.

"Good-by," I said, and knelt.

I would have given him a decent burial, had I the time, but Patrick, like my father, cared little what happened to his carcass after the soul had fled. And Ireland was demanding justice for the living, not rites for the dead. Distantly to the west I saw the body of his dead horse mounding in the breakers. Mounting Mia, I galloped away to the east, through the dunes and along the flinted road to St-Valery.

It was nearly eight o'clock by the time I had skirted St-Valery and reached the crossroads on the Abbeville road, and a September sun that had forgotten the season was slanting swords of incinerating fire on the gay, autumn country. I reined in Mia and she stamped impatiently around the road, making enough commotion to raise the French cavalry; so, fearfully, I led her into a little wooded glade beside a stream. Of the Irish patriot there was no sign; nor did I ever meet him. Disconsolate, knowing that the coach of Monsieur Le Garde and Captain Wentworth was due within half an hour, I wandered the glade, easing my rapier in the scabbard and priming my two pistols.

Of a sudden I came upon a little statue of Our Lady among the trees, the friend of my dead mother, she being a Catholic. Mia watched me intently as I knelt beside the wayside shrine, picking wild roses and placing them in Mary's hands, which were outstretched to me. To this Mother I prayed for the strength to do what Ireland claimed as my duty. I also prayed that she might intercede for my life, for it is well known that Jesus, her Son, listens to her advice. Not that I was afraid of death. But it was necessary for me to live to protect a greater life, that of Theobald Wolfe Tone.

I was just crossing myself in respect to my mother when I felt the needle point of a weapon pierce the skin of my shoulder blade.

"Keep still," said a voice, heavy with a French accent.

I kept still.

The man behind me chuckled low in his throat. "Oho! It is wonderful indeed to see an Englishman on his knees!"

I did not move but said, "You're on the wrong nationality, man. But give me half a chance and I'll have you on your knees. Or do you always fight behind a man's back?"

"Arrah! It talks! *Allez oop!*" The rapier point shifted to my hat; with a flick of the wrist he sent it flying. "Next time it will be your head, Englishman. Stand, *stand!*"

I rose, weighing him. Hands on hips he stood before me, the point of his rapier on the grass in front of him. He was a big man, and handsome, and in his dark, Latin face there was the stamp of the Spanish grandee, but I knew him for

French. There was about him a freebooting arrogance—a soldier of fortune if ever I saw one.

"You have money, Monsieur?" he asked.

"Yes, I have money." He was being a nuisance and I wanted him out of the way as quickly as possible, for soon the coach would come. If I was to be outnumbered, the sooner this one went the better. He said, flicking the lace at his wrist, "You come from English fishing boat, so you bring English sovereigns, eh?"

"What makes you think I came from a boat?"

He spread his hands, his white teeth appearing in his dark face. "Because I see. Two fools I see, on horses, swimming ashore at Pointe le Renne. One, he is drowned, also the horse, and I am sad for him. The other, he swim ashore on this very fine horse." He indicated Mia grazing nearby. "It is sadder still, Monsieur, but my horse is old and yours is young. Five golden English sovereigns you give me, or I take your horse." He bowed low. "And accept the apologies of François Malon."

An idea came to me. "You are a soldier of fortune, Monsieur Malon?"

"Once, perhaps, but now I am a horse thief, though not quite without honor."

I said, "I will give you ten sovereigns of English gold if you will fight for me. I have enemies, and soon . . ."

He grinned wider and came close. "And what if I am killed in this fighting? What good to me is ten gold pieces if I am dead?"

"That is the luck of a soldier of fortune," I said.

He shrugged. "Perhaps I fight you instead, then I will have the horse and all your gold pieces."

"If you fight me I will kill you, have no doubt."

This put him double, fist up and shrieking with laughter. "You kill me? I, François Malon, the best rapier north and south of Chantilly? And you a stripling boy-man!"

On a sudden breath of the wind I heard galloping hoofs and the unmistakable clatter of a coach, but the Frenchman seemed not to have heard this.

I said, "Come, sir, enough of this. If I cannot buy your sword I will give you ten sovereigns to be gone. One day, who knows, you might help me. If you are the best rapier around Chantilly, which is the school of the rapier, you are far too good for me." I took out my purse and tossed it to him, and he snatched it in mid-air and thrust it into his doublet.

"You are up to something, Englishman," he said, his smile gone.

I said, levelly, "You are half a man, a wayside footpad, and I wish you gone, for I have business on my hands."

But he did not move. His dark eyes wandered lazily over me and he smiled. "I do not trust you, Englishman. Chantilly is the schoolhouse of the French rapier, and you are carrying one. If you know of Chantilly, Monsieur, then you are not such a fool with the blade."

"I have heard talk of Chantilly," I said. "This is my father's rapier, but I am not a fighting man."

"I do not intend to wait and see!" Wandering away, he whistled up a bony old nag, swung himself into the saddle, and grinned down at me. There was about him a devil-may-care charm, and for all his being a thief and a rogue, I was beginning to like him. He said, "If you are a white-feather swordsman, there is no risk to me. Now I have the money. Later, when it is spent on wining and wenching, I will come back for the horse." Bending, he speared my hat from the grass and placed it neatly on my head with his rapier. "*Au revoir*, Englishman. One moment you threaten to kill me, next moment you pay me for nothing. My mother would tell me not to trust such a situation." He spurred hard, his gay laughter echoing in the glade as he galloped away.

I wished him to the devil for a thieving vagabond. He had gone not a moment too soon: I could hear the coach coming plainly now, and it was astonishing to me that he had not heard it too. Unscrewing my powder flask, I ran a thin trail of gunpowder from the roadside ditch to the middle of the road, emptying the remainder into a little pile. And as I smacked Mia away into cover and leaped into the shelter of the ditch, the coach carrying Le Garde and Captain Wentworth came rattling and swaying around the bend toward me, with the two horses galloping like creatures demented in a thunder of wheels and the coachman's whip curling high above them. My heart began to pound against my shirt. It was a big risk, yet I had no option but to take it. Le Garde, according to Caine Adams, was a

duelist and therefore a man of courage. Captain Wentworth was a professional fighting man, one trained in the
tough schools of England. And there was also the driver.
It was three against one.

If the life of the patriot Wolfe Tone was to be saved, I
would have to do it alone. The coach was twenty yards
away now. Bending, I lit the gunpowder fuse.

I always pitied the terror of horses in the blaze of a
gunpowder ambush.

These two great creatures shrieked and went high
before the blaze, hind legs skidding sparks, forelegs pawing.
And as the weight of the coach impelled them through the
flash they leaped in the shafts, cantering sideways, spilling
the driver from his seat. I had a quick glimpse of his
bearded face, mouth open to scream in the second before
the coach, blundering sideways along the flinted road,
slowly came to a halt, lurched on two wheels, and lazily
overturned. There was a crash of splintering glass. Silence,
momentarily. Then faintly I heard the thudding hoofs of
the horses who had broken free and were galloping over
the field beyond with reins, traces, and broken shafts
trailing behind them.

With rapier in one hand and pistol in the other, I darted
over to the coach, which lay on its side. And as I reached
it a hand came upward through the shattered glass, feeling
for the handle of the door. Standing well back on the
broken shafts, I heaved the door open and then ducked to

a blinding flash as a pistol was fired. Momentarily shaken, I fell backward, and Captain Wentworth was instantly through the door, flinging the discharged pistol at my head, but his aim was bad. Now he was upon me as I struggled up, trying to regain my dropped pistol. His oncoming charge bore me backward, and I struck the gravel of the road with a force that pumped the breath out of my body. Somehow I clambered upright and blocked his first thrust with the sword. We circled, staring at each other, weapons out, in the manner of duelists. But this, I knew, could be no fair fight. In panic I was watching the door of the overturned coach. The bloody face of Le Garde appeared, then his shoulders; and I saw him steady a double-barreled pistol on the smashed woodwork.

"Aho! On guard, man, *guard!*" Wentworth thrust again, and I parried him, standing my ground, keeping his body protectively between Le Garde, who was waiting to fire, and my own. In sudden anger Wentworth came again, feinting and thrusting with the speed of light. Fine and strong he looked with his bright hair falling over his forehead and his eyes sparkling at the prospect of a fight, and I realized as I rallied and drove him backward that, dressed in his French uniform, we could pass for twins. The committee, in selecting me to impersonate him in the English spy ring, had done its job well.

Now he came again with a wide grin of confidence, driving me before him with a skill that surprised me, but he opened his guard at the last moment and I thrust him.

With astonishing alacrity, he side-stepped the blade, but slipped to one knee on the wet grass. Seeing me exposed, Le Garde fired from the coach, and as Wentworth leaped again to face me, the ball took him square, high on the head. He stiffened, frozen by the impact, and his eyes opened wide at me, as if in question. Then he fell, face down, dead at my feet. And the moment he fell Le Garde, the target of my body open to him, fired the second barrel. The ball missed my head by inches, whining away into the trees behind me. I crouched to rush him and was struck from behind, for I had forgotten the coachman.

Turning to the impact of the blow, I fell, and the world about me shattered into nothingness. I saw, in the second before unconsciousness claimed me, the coachman standing over me with his whip-butt raised, his brutal, bearded face peering down.

"Shall I kill him, Monsieur Le Garde?" he cried.

Captured

When I returned to consciousness I found that my hands and feet were brutally tied and that, to my astonishment, I was upon Mia's back. My arms were strapped behind me at the elbows, my ankles were tied to her stirrups, the ropes running under her belly to keep me on the saddle. I drooped forward in this cruel position, jogging painfully to her every footstep, though I swear to this day she was walking as evenly as a horse could walk, to save me pain.

"He is coming alive, Monsieur Le Garde!" cried the coachman.

Blood was congealed on my shirt as I dragged up my aching body to face him, and more was on my face and hands. I realized that this man had beaten me after striking me down.

"You wish to stop and question him, Monsieur Le Garde?"

"At the next bridle path, man. We will first get clear of the road."

Le Garde spurred his horse, and I saw now that both

were riding the coach horses bareback. Across the back of the coachman's mount, the body of Captain Wentworth dangled face down, boots and hands hanging loose in a fantastic indignity of death.

"Give him half an hour with me and I'll get the truth of him." The coachman laughed cruelly. "And after that, I say finish him!" He spurred beside me, reached out, and grabbed my hair, twisting up my face to his.

"That is the last thing we do, my friend," replied Le Garde. He had a fine, aristocratic dignity despite the cuts and humped bruises on his face caused by the crash. "I have a friend who will know what to do with an Irish spy." He smiled into my face. "Ah, yes, Monsieur, we were expecting you and your famous Patrick Hays, but I vow we thought you had given up the chase after he was drowned."

"I bet he don't know how you come about that, your honor," cried the coachman in his rough patois.

"Do you believe your mastermind Caine Adams to be foolproof, young man? If you do, then you are a bigger fool than he. The man with the lantern, for instance; you thought him an Irish patriot, yet he was in our pay."

"Did his job well, that one," said the coachman, giving me an evil grin.

"Indeed, he did," said Le Garde. "He guided Marcel Robet to a point on the estuary where only fools and fishes can swim, and reported to me that you lost your companion . . ."

"And Marcel Robet?" I asked, turning to him.

"Marcel Robet is employed directly by Petit Pierre and receives his pay from your enemies. My good friend Marcel is in a most fortunate position, John Regan. He receives two salaries—one from us and one from the Rebel Committee of the United Irishmen."

I had already guessed this, and said, in wonder, "You even know my name."

"One of your rebel leaders talked before he died. We in London knew you were to ambush this coach and impersonate us before you and Hays knew it yourselves."

I was scarcely listening. A coldness was growing in me despite the fever of my wounds. Caine Adams, in his blindness and great age, had miscalculated the enemy for the first and last time. Patrick was already dead; soon I would die, too. But the thought of Caine Adams dying at the hands of the double agent Marcel Robet was almost more than I could bear.

"It is needless to add, perhaps," said Le Garde, "that your beloved and revered Caine Adams will never again see Ireland."

"God help him," I said bitterly and bowed my head.

"And God help you, Monsieur John Regan, when we get you to Paris. Petit Pierre, like me, stands against the new *republique* and your rebellious Ireland. Under his leadership the aristocracy of France will rise again!" His voice rose to a fanatical cry. "And with England as our ally we shall smash the power of the rebel people who have brought us to disgrace and death. The guillotines will be built again in the cities of France, and they shall drink the blood of the rebel swine and their leader, Napoleon Bonaparte!"

"Aye, aye!" muttered the coachman, beating his breast. He raised his dissolute face to the sun. "You think the Black Midget will put this one's neck to the blade, Monsieur Le Garde?"

"If I know Petit Pierre, he will reserve this one for a different fate—the recruiter of the Spanish galleys is his very special friend. You heard what I said, John Regan?"

I gave him a wink and a happy grin. Inwardly, I felt physically sick with fear.

"You still have to get me to Paris, Monsieur," I said.

"That will be the easiest part of this unhappy affair," said Monsieur Le Garde. "But the unhappiest part for you will be the next ten minutes, for it is important that my coachman gets every word of truth from you before we start for Paris." He jogged along beside me, smiling into my face. "My friend and companion, Captain Wentworth, is dead. We were ordered to kill Wolfe Tone and have come from London for that purpose. Petit Pierre has pledged our safe passage; now we will have to give a full explanation. I want the name of every United Irishman involved in this affair. I want to know the names of the Frenchmen supporting Wolfe Tone in this proposed French invasion of your country, the number of the invasion force, the names of the ships that will carry them, and their port of departure from France. Lastly, I want the date of this invasion, and I want this most of all."

"I do not know any of these things," I replied. "And if I knew I would not tell you."

"That," said Le Garde, "remains to be seen." He turned to the coachman. "The prisoner is yours, coachman. Do with him as you will."

"Monsieur Le Garde," cried the coachman, "this is a tremendous honor!" Seizing Mia's bridle, he led us off the road. Distantly, spearing the blue sky, I saw the church spires of Abbeville, and great rays of sunlight were shafting down from a rent in the clouds, and I could have wept for the beauty of it. All the loveliness of this September morning seemed to grow about me; the hand of God seemed to be moving over the earth with a great compassion. And as Le Garde led me to the place of torture myriad dewdrops sparkled and flashed from every leaf and blade, and I smelled the sweet-sour earth smell of this lovely place—in the land my father loved.

"This is good," said the coachman, rubbing his hands. "I am an expert, Monsieur Le Garde. In this I am excellent —not too far from the road to make a long walk, not too close to Abbeville to hear the Irish scream."

Shifting awkwardly in the saddle, Le Garde said, "I—I will ride down this path, man. In half an hour I will be back, and I want the truth of him. I want the truth, coachman, every word. But kill him, and you account to me for it. His life is loaned to you; it belongs to Petit Pierre in Paris."

As he reined away, I called, "Stay and watch, Monsieur Le Garde. If you employ such scum to do your dirty work, the least you can do is to stay and watch."

Over his shoulder he said, "I will return in half an hour," and I cried to him: "Of the two, you are the more disgusting."

The coachman approached me.

Involuntarily, I shivered at his touch.

"You afraid of me, Irish boy?"

Your manhood will come when you need it most, said my father. Mia, tethered nearby, watched the scene with dark, liquid eyes. The coachman, kneeling, began to light a fire, grunting at me through the smoke.

And, above me, in a pattern of branches, a lark nicked and dived, singing with joy.

Liberté, Égalité, Fraternité

Standing at the fire, the coachman turned to the sound of hoofs, whispering, "Monsieur Le Garde, is that you?" Then he rose, shouting, "Who is there?" He picked up his pistol.

The glade echoed his voice, and then I heard faint hoofbeats crunching through the crisp refuse of autumn. And I saw in the coachman's face the growing panic of a man confronted with an unknown enemy. For there was in these woods a tainted loneliness; as if the gnarled trees, dumb witnesses to my coming pain, might suddenly turn to ghosts, ready to pounce and strangle with fingers of green ivy and black twig.

"Who—who is it?" asked the coachman hoarsely.

I twisted upward, raising my head from the ground.

A skinny, riderless horse was wandering toward us through a clearing, and the coachman visibly relaxed, dropping the pistol. It was a mistake, for when he turned back to me he came face to face with François Malon, the soldier of fortune.

"*Bonjour*, Messieurs!" cried Malon, and the coachman staggered backward.

Fists on his hips, Malon swaggered to the fire. With his cockade hat on the back of his head and his rapier tenting his cloak behind him, he wandered in toward us. Big and arrogant he looked, his smile wide and happy, and he shouted joyfully, "This fire I smell half the way to Chantilly. François Malon, I said, somebody will soon be cooking breakfast, eh?"

"What—what do you want with us?" whispered the coachman, and he shot a nervous glance down the path where Le Garde had gone. Malon spread his hands.

"Only to eat, Monsieur. It is little to ask—a bite and sup for a fellow traveler." Suddenly, as if he had just noticed me lying there, he bowed low, his cockade hat sweeping the grass at my feet. "*Mon Dieu!* What is this, a man tied?" He drew his rapier and wandered around the terrified coachman. "This is not hospitable, Monsieur. How can your friend eat breakfast if his hands are tied? Where are you headed?"

"Paris," whispered the coachman, gripping his fingers.

Malon jerked his thumb at me. "And him, too? How can he ride a horse with his feet tied together, tell me?"

I said evenly, "A hundred guineas, Malon, if you free me."

"Free you? And why should I do that? *Mon ami!* You ask me to interfere between friendly travelers? There must be good reason for you to be captive." He swung to the coachman. "This fellow is your prisoner, good sir?"

The man straightened. "I carry him to Paris to face the justice of the people. He is an enemy of France!" He flashed a look down the glade. I wondered if the freebooter knew that Le Garde was close; that I had another enemy who would not think twice about shooting him in the back.

Malon replied, "If he is an enemy of the French *republique*, then you should shoot him and have done with it. *Voilà!* Who have we here?" His eyes alighted on the body of Captain Wentworth. "One dead already? Here is a very strange situation. You are a traveling undertaker, man. And an English captain, too! This is excellent, my friend. If I had my way I would shoot every one of them."

He had turned his back on the coachman. Seeing his opportunity, the man dashed to the fire, where his pistol was lying, but François Malon, as if inadvertently, stepped backward and put his heel upon it. The coachman hesitated, then slowly rose. A new panic was growing in his face at this play of cat and mouse. Going to Mia, Malon gently brushed her flank.

"This," said Malon, "is a very fine horse, and I have come for her, as I promised." He grinned happily down at me. "Today is excellent. I am handed gold and a fine mare, what more could a man ask, Monsieur? I do not even have to tie you—this has been done for me." He swung onto Mia's back and reached forward and untethered her, crying to the coachman, "This mare, sir, she was promised me by the prisoner you have. You have no objection to my taking her?"

The coachman beamed. "Not in the least, Monsieur—take her and welcome. Good day, sir!"

"And good day to you, Monsieur," said Malon, dismounting. Drawing his pistol, he cocked it and slowly approached the trembling man. "I think I smell a rat," said he, and I saw that his demeanor had changed. "In fact, Monsieur, I smell two rats. Rats who tie a helpless man—rats who light a fire, yet do not cook breakfast. No, I do not like this situation—neither would my poor old mother." He added softly, "There is an evil here, Monsieur. If you fight and kill my young friend, this is all right, but I do not like him tied and helpless. I, François Malon, cannot bear the indignity of the helpless man, nor do I care to see a gentleman in the hands of a cutthroat."

I cried again, "A hundred sovereigns from the United Irishmen, Malon, if you set me free."

In sudden terror the coachman shouted hoarsely, "Set him free, sir, and you will answer to Monsieur Le Garde. Five hundred lashes and the Spanish galleys if you lift a finger to help the Irishman!" He shouted in anger, "Be gone, before Le Garde comes back and kills you!"

"I doubt if that will happen," said Malon. "Five minutes ago I let the daylight through Monsieur Le Garde for the traitor that he is. Long live the new *republique!*"

The coachman gasped, "He is dead?"

"Certainly. For too long I have watched him coming and going in the service of English spies, the enemies of France. That rapier at your belt, man—how did you come by it?"

I cried, "It is stolen from me, Malon."

"I thought I recognized it." Bending, he picked up the coachman's pistol and thrust it into his belt. Kneeling beside me, he cut the rope that tied me and then drew his own rapier and pushed it into my hand. I rose unsteadily.

"*Liberté, Égalité, Fraternité,*" said he. "If you are the sword I think you are we will drink a toast to you in Chantilly." He jerked his thumb at the coachman and turned away. "Meanwhile be of service to beloved France and save this devil from the terror of the guillotine."

I gripped the rapier and moved toward him. "Draw," I said.

And as the coachman drew and raised his right hand for balance, François Malon cried, "I leave you to your destiny, Irishman. Le Garde's stallion will suffice me for a while, but next time we meet I will have the mare." And he strolled down the bridle path without a backward look.

"On guard!" cried the coachman, and rushed.

But he had not been trained in the school of Chantilly; at the second attack I ran him through. Then, kneeling, I checked Captain Wentworth's identity papers and stripped his body of his French officer's uniform. Swiftly changing into these clothes, I buried my own in a ditch of leaves beside the Englishman's body. Leaving that glade of death, I spurred Mia along the road to Abbeville, and the late afternoon was sticky with heat as I took her over the fields to bypass Amiens.

The moon was rising like a ghostly galleon by the time I trotted a weary Mia into a lovely little hamlet east of Beauvais and went in search of the inn Caine Adams called the Creton Belle. I found it almost at once at the end of a sweet French lane, its black-and-white half-timbered gables shouting its link with England, its leaded windows pouring bright swords of light over the dusty road that led to Compiègne. Tethering Mia at the entrance, I entered boldly, as befits an armed traveler.

The taprooms of wayside inns, whether in France or Ireland, are much alike; human beings react to a stranger in much the same way, whatever their nationality. And the tap of the Creton Belle was no exception. All heads turned to me as I entered, the suspicious eyes of the men taking in every detail of my dress. But many strangers were traveling abroad in France at this time—men from the new French empire won under Napoleon, soldiers of the Italian dependencies, and the mercenaries of Savoy and the Rhineland. Many of them could not speak French at all, but worked by the language of signs. So my poor French, for all my shame of it, served me well.

"Good evening," I said at the tap counter. Two big Corsican officers raised their tanned faces to mine, and I turned, bowing to their table. Instantly, they were on their feet, bowing back. At the back of the little, low-ceilinged room, the riffraff of the French barricades raised expressionless eyes. In a corner a wrecked soldier, the refuse of Bonaparte, raised a flask of wine to his pallid lips, his hand shaking as with an ague.

"You travel far, Monsieur?" asked the landlord. Bald as an egg and thin as a leek, he gripped his bony hands.

"From St-Valery."

In a corner a beggar was playing a flute in the folds of his rags, and his little mongrel dog, her ears pierced with bright red ribbons, danced on her hind legs in the sawdust, bowing to the customers one by one. I recognized the melody instantly; it was an old English air.

"How long are you staying, Monsieur?"

"Only tonight. A meal for me and fodder for my horse?"

I glanced over my shoulder at the musician. His eyes, as if glazed in his ravaged face, were fixed on mine, and the mongrel danced on, bowing, bowing.

"Two francs. Pay now, Monsieur."

I did so, silently cursing François Malon for leaving me short. Unexpectedly, the landlord said, "We can only lend you the bed, Monsieur. We expected two gentlemen from St-Valery many hours ago, but they have not come. If they come later, you give up the bed, eh?"

"*Oui*, Monsieur. Of course."

"We keep a very good stable—all over Oise it is said that I keep a clean stable, you understand?" He added, "Even Jean Le Garde says so, you hear?"

"Perfectly," I replied. "It won't be the first time I have slept with a horse." I wondered if he was telling me that he knew Monsieur Le Garde.

"Madame will show you the room, Monsieur."

I bowed to him. "Thank you, but first I will attend to my mare."

"The horse is the legs of a man," said he. "It is right that you see to her first." He added, "Go through the kitchen to get to the yard."

The old English air from the beggar's flute followed me out into the night. Mia was stamping impatiently on the cobbles, for my father always used to see to her before he bedded himself. To humor her I gave her the handful of sugar I had stolen coming through the kitchen, and she nibbled at my fingers for thanks, shoving and barging me for more while I led her into the stall. There, I set before her a pail of bright spring water. When she had drunk her fill, I put a nose bag on her big enough to sink an elephant. "And you be ready to hoof on a moment's notice," I whispered, and gripped her mane, looking into the black shadows of the yard. Unaccountably I was ill at ease. Despite the loveliness of the September night of moon and gossamer, I sensed in it a withdrawn evil. There was no sound in that yard but wind-whisper and the unending music of the flute, and the music crept about me, filling me with an unnamed premonition of disaster.

Soon a man with a shattered face, the agent of the Black Midget, would come and question me. He would assume me to be Captain Paul Wentworth; he would question me on the whereabouts of Monsieur Le Garde and the coachman. And all this I would have to answer to his satisfaction. I was sick at heart. For I had no doubt at all that the Creton Belle was a hotbed of English espionage, that armed men were stationed there who could be called upon to effect my arrest at the very first suspicion. This is when the actor in the game of spying is demanded, and I was no actor. This was Patrick's role, after his vast experience in the spy rings, but I must play it, for he was dead.

A man with a shattered face . . . There was something unearthly about it, inhuman.

I shuddered, like a man standing on the edge of his grave.

The Man with the Shattered Face

It is the unknown that I find hard to bear—the whisper in the darkness, the cold breath of wind in an airless place, the hand that moves over the face in sleep. All my life I have been the same. Terror for me lies not in the seen enemy nor in the face of death at odds of ten to one. It lies in the unnamed, the unseen, the creatures of the night, the things that creep.

From the moment I entered the Creton Belle, I had felt this fear, a foreboding that grew about me with a strangle hold.

Now I lay in a little attic bedroom and watched the moon sliding in a blaze of silver across the leaded window. The inn was silent; the revelers on the road to Compiègne had long since taken to their beds. The flute of the beggar was stilled. Unbreathing, with its dormers glinting at the moon, the inn steamed in the September mist.

Something moved in the little room. I stiffened. Sweat broke cold on my face and ran in little chilling streams over my body. I sat up in the bed.

"Who is there?" I said.

No answer came, yet on my oath I could hear breathing. The wind moved on the white road outside; autumn leaves tapped at the window like crisp, dead moths; faintly I heard Mia stamping in her stable. I sank back again on the pillow, every nerve tuned to fever pitch in that tingling silence. Suddenly, angered by my own fearfulness, I sprang from the bed and went to the window. Nothing stirred over the moon-silvered country. It was indescribably beautiful, but strange and empty.

Creeping back to the bed, like a man afraid to disturb the ghosts, I lay in a fitful drowse. I was awakened almost instantly, it seemed, by the knowledge of a presence: a sense so powerful that it sat me up, hands gripping the bed.

A man was standing by the window. Unmoving he stood, as if carved from stone.

In that blinding moment of wakefulness, I could not see his face. For the moon was behind him, etching him into total blackness. And even as I gathered myself for the attack, all my fears vanished by the proof that he was mortal, for he said, "Do not shout, Monsieur Wentworth. I beg you not to shout." But his voice was scarcely the voice of a human being, the tone harsh, like the croak of a raven.

"Who—who are you?" I rose from the bed, taking a step toward him.

"And stay where you are, Captain; I beg you stay."

I had to concentrate hard to understand his words. "What do you want of me?"

"It is what you want of me, surely. Where is Jean Le Garde, Monsieur?"

I said, peering at him through the darkness, "You are my contact at the Creton Belle."

"I am he, but no man knows my name," he whispered. "I come by night, as always. In darkness I come, so that those more fortunate than I shall not know revulsion."

I bowed my head, for the moon, in sudden flight, had passed its light over his features. This was the man with the shattered face. I whispered assent.

"Do not pity me," said he. "Where is Jean Le Garde? My instructions are to deal with him, your guide."

I faced him, steeling myself for the lie. It is unfortunate that in a noble occupation such as this, one is not trained in the art of lying, for a lie, in espionage, can mean the difference between life and death.

The moon was full on my face as I said, gripping my hands behind me, "Jean Le Garde, my friend and companion, is dead. This morning, outside St-Valery, we were attacked by two United Irishmen. Le Garde and the coachman were shot. I managed to escape." I stared directly at the broken face before me. "Jean Le Garde, in an act of bravery, dismounted one of the assailants and, in doing so, he died. I managed to mount the Irishman's horse, and I galloped here directly, as instructed by London."

There was a silence, broken only by his ragged breathing. He said, "You have proof of identity, Captain Wentworth?"

"I have my passport. Here." I stopped, reached inside my tunic, and offered the passport I had taken from the dead body of Captain Paul Wentworth.

The agent held it up to the light of the window, and I caught a glimpse of his face again. Never have I seen such a total violation: only his eyes remained, large and strangely beautiful. Below these eyes was nothing that resembled a face. For the cannon ball that had preserved him for this living death had passed red hot across nose and mouth and chin, and he was found three days later in the tangled wreckage of a French frigate—a lone French frigate which had the audacity to tangle with an English ship of the line. And the embalming sea, by some strange chemistry, had cauterized his wounds. Now all there remained to this man, said Caine Adams, was a double, vicious hatred: hatred of Bonaparte, who was the cause of this mutilation, and hatred of the sea for this sentence to human rejection.

Beware of this hatred; beware of this untidy man, said Caine Adams. He is the most dangerous milestone on your road to Petit Pierre, the spy leader.

Now the man said hoarsely, "The passport is in order, but it is not enough." He bowed slightly. "I am responsible for the safety of this mission. You will answer some questions?"

"Of course. But speak carefully; my French is not good."

He moved into the shadows again. "Your parents. Alive or dead, sir?"

"Alive and well," I answered.

"Where were you born?"

"In the village of Alton, in Hampshire."

"And you were raised there?"

It was a trap, and I knew it. Inwardly I blessed Caine Adams for briefing me so well. "No, Monsieur," I replied. "I was raised in County Cork in Ireland by Mrs. Mary Jennings, my aunt. Hence my Irish accent."

"Why was this so? Your parents live in England and you were raised in Ireland by an aunt?" His eyes shone at me from the black desecration of his face. I hesitated, lowering my head, and he said, "I ask you again, Monsieur. Why were you not raised by your parents?"

I replied softly, "Because I am not the legitimate child of my father, sir. This is my shame, and I beg you to respect this confidence."

It was disgusting to have to lie like this: to open the grave of an English officer and peer into his soul. Even in service to a beloved country it turned my stomach, but it convinced my questioner, as Caine Adams had assured me.

The man said, "Accept my apologies for such an inquisition, Captain Wentworth. You will appreciate that, in the interests of Royal France, I have to be quite certain of your identity."

"Of course," I said.

His hand went out and I gripped it. The skin, the knuckles were amazingly smooth to the touch, and I shivered involuntarily. He added, "Now repeat your mission in this country."

"I am to assassinate Theobald Wolfe Tone, the United Irishman who, with Commodore Bompart under Napoleon, is planning to take a French invasion force to the shores of Ireland."

"Only this?"

"I am also to learn and report to the English espionage under the command of Monsieur Petit Pierre of Bastille the full plans of the invasion force—its strength, the date of sailing, the names and number of warships. When this is reported I am to return immediately to London and report the same to the English government."

To my surprise, he bowed. "You are a brave man, Captain Wentworth. Petit Pierre will approve of you, have my assurance." He handed me an envelope. "Take this letter to him in person and you will receive from him instructions concerning how you are to enter Wolfe Tone's service and gain his confidence. You know the address of Pierre?"

"Cellar number sixteen," I replied, "Rue de Victoire, Bastille Square."

"Correct. You need a new horse, Captain Wentworth? Or will you take the same coach horse you have been using since you were ambushed with Jean Le Garde?"

It was yet another trap. I replied casually, "The mare I am using is not a French coach horse, Monsieur. I took her from one of the Irishmen during the attack."

He nodded, and had he possessed a face, he would have been smiling. "Of course," he said. "I had forgotten. I checked her in the stable earlier. Being an expert in bloodstock, I was naturally interested in her origins. She is not of French blood."

"Irish, I would hazard a guess, Monsieur?"

He paused at the door. "Irish more than likely."

He went the way he had come, like a wraith of darkness, his feet quite soundless on the narrow stairs.

The envelope was stark white in my hand. In it, I knew, was the secret of my future. Life, or death?

A Little Dancing Dog

When I took my leave of the landlord of the Creton Belle the next morning the taproom was empty of guests. Only two French soldiers remained, sprawled together over a table in the aftermath of a drunken sleep. One raised bloodshot eyes at me as I went to the counter. The landlord asked, "You sleep well, Monsieur?" His eyes bulged at me with the blank stare of a squirrel.

"Very well," I replied, and glanced around the room again. "The two gentlemen you expected from St-Valery did not arrive?"

He spread his hands. "They did not come, and we are amazed. Only two days ago Monsieur Le Garde wrote that he would be arriving with a guest." He put before me the bread and cheese his wife had prepared. "You eat on the road, then? It would be simpler to stay for breakfast —the price is the same."

I shook my head. "I am making an early start, Monsieur. I have to be in Paris by this time tomorrow, and my horse is already tired."

"You came yesterday from St-Valery, sir?" asked a voice, and I turned at the inn door. The beggar was sitting in a dim corner. Nestling in his lap was the little dancing dog, and sticking out of his rags was his flute. His red mouth appeared like a wound in his bearded face.

I smiled at him. "Yes, I came from St-Valery."

The landlord bristled, shouting at the beggar, "You keep a civil tongue, beggar, and don't make bold with a paying gentleman!"

"Just wondering, lan'lord—no harm in wondering. Perhaps the fine gentleman got a sight of Jean Le Garde and his guest, since he also came from St-Valery." His French, like mine, was uncertain.

I began to curse myself for engaging this one in polite conversation.

"Not a glimpse," I answered.

"There now, not a glimpse—d'ye hear that, gutter-snipe?" bawled the landlord in admonition. To me he said, "Come again, sir, no offense intended. Good day to ye."

I was ill at ease as I went to the stable and saddled Mia, who was still dozing as if tomorrow would do. And she moved over her hindquarters as I entered the stall, pinning me against the wall, for this was a game she played if I came too early.

"Get over, ye idiot," I whispered.

At this she looked over her shoulder and snorted and leaned harder, but I fought myself free and got the saddle across her, and she kept bringing up her hind hoof, making it awkward to tighten the girths.

"Will you behave, ye daft rapscallion!" I breathed. "If we don't get on the road to Paris this minute we'll never see the skies over Wexford again, you included!"

I was still kneeling beside her working on the girths when the pretty little dancing dog came bowling up as large as life, and Mia did a sniff and snort as the dog danced around on her hind legs, stretching up to kiss Mia's muzzle. It was prettier still, but it told me two things.

The little dancing dog was very used to horses. What's more, if she was here, then her master could not be very far away.

And in the next stall a big black horse was looking over the bar, very interested in the proceedings. Seeing him suddenly, the little dog leaped high in a paroxysm of joy, and the black horse whinnied his reply.

Friends, these, and companions: without a doubt this was the beggar's horse. And from what I had just heard, he was no ordinary beggar. His French, accurate enough for a traveler, nevertheless had the ring of Killarney to me.

So I closed Mia's stable door and climbed over the bar, dropping down beside the black horse. I stroked his mane and gave him a bit of sugar I had been saving for Mia. And while he was enjoying it, I knelt, lifting his foreleg. With my knife I pried up his shoe and dropped a tiny flint under it. Then I put my face against his and stroked his nose.

"Sorry, lad," I said.

There were some queer old characters staying at the Creton Belle from what Caine Adams had told me. But one thing was sure. If I was going to have followers down the road to Paris I was drawing the line at an Irish beggar with a dancing dog.

I took to the fields outside Beauvais and, north of Pontoise, crossed the Oise. It was about midday when I trotted into the market town of Chantilly, giving a fleeting but affectionate thought to the vagabond François Malon, for this was his home.

Mia went lame on me two miles southwest of beautiful Chantilly, and when I led her into an abandoned quarry clear of the road she held up her hind leg and pushed it at me, giving me a look to kill. Getting out my penknife, I pried up her shoe. Sure enough, there was a tiny flint cutting into her foot, about the same size as I had used to hobble the beggar's horse back at the Creton Belle. And this, when you come to think of it, was poetic justice of a sort.

Resting Mia in this quiet place, I took my sleeping roll off her saddle and tethered her near some lush grass to graze. It was then that I remembered my parents. Always, before I slept, I prayed for them. In that deserted place, I knelt for my mother, she being a Catholic. After this, I spoke from the Book of Common Prayer for my father, who was a Protestant. I also prayed for my beloved

Ireland and took from my doublet pocket a little clod of earth and grass which I had taken from a field in County Wexford. This earth I held in my cupped hands, and the blades of grass, once green, were now withered—as the soul of my people was being withered in the flames of English oppression.

I was lying with my head on the bedroll when Mia stamped her foot on the grass nearby. Instantly I drew my pistol.

Before me, on her hind legs, sat the beggar's little dog. And beyond her, leading his fine black horse into the quarry, was the beggar himself.

"Don't come any nearer," I said, leveling my pistol at him as he stood there.

"Are ye shooting the wee dog, then?" he asked in English.

"I'm shooting you, if you make so much as a single move."

For an answer, he pushed his moleskin hat back on his head. "Is this the way ye greet a compatriot of the great and holy country, then?" he asked, in a broad Killarney accent.

"It's the way I'm treatin' you, till I get the measure o' this," I replied.

"Well, boyo, until ye get the measure of us, would ye like the wee bitch to do a dance for ye, for she's aching to do so. An' she dances that much better to the melody o' the Killarney flute."

I grinned at him. There was a blaze of goodness in him
as he took off the beard, and a fine handsome young chap
he was beneath the whiskers.

"Start fluting," I said. "We'll give the fair country of
France a good Irish reel and a dancing dog to remember
us by."

"Consider it done," said he, and squatted by the horse's
feet and raised the flute to his lips, saying, "And not a
move out o' ye' me boy, or the gentleman'll have the pair
of us with the same fist. He's no great shakes at lovin'
anyone, for all he's Irish. Didn't he put a flint under your
shoe? And you an innocent horse who never harmed a
livin' creature!"

"Which is what you did to my mare, too," I said.

"Och, what's a couple of flints between Irish friends?"
he asked. "I've been wandering the fair land of France for
long, but it isn't a patch on the beauty of Ireland, and I'm
going back soon."

"Will your beard be on or off when ye return to the
holy land?" I asked over the leveled pistol.

"Off more than likely, for though they're partial to
fluters with beards in France, they don't care much for
'em in Derry."

"What are ye doing in France, at a time when your
country needs ye?"

"Och," said he, "the country might need me, but I don't
need the country. I'm a Wexford man, d'ye see. And if I
was in Wexford now the English would be after me scalp

if I was a patriot rebel. And if I wasn't a rebel me own flesh and blood would be belting me at a tree for consorting with the landlords and the English redcoats. What's a fella to do? So I sailed for fair France."

"Before the rebellion?" I asked.

"Aye, for sure, man. You're not gettin' me losing me head in that palaver."

"You're worse than useless," I said, lowering the pistol.

"Am I now? And where does that put you, man? What are you up to—rovin' the roads of a foreign country— unless you're up to no good?"

"My business," I said.

"Did ye not have sight or smell of Jean Le Garde and his English guest, then, along the road from St-Valery?"

"I don't know what you're talking about," I muttered.

He shrugged. "I was just wondering. You see, there's some queer company inhabiting the Creton Belle. There's a fella there, for instance, who's got his wits but lacks a face. He was expecting two chaps to meet him there last evening—one was a man called Jean Le Garde, the other was a guest, according to the landlord. He's a fine gab on him, that landlord."

"Aye, go on," I said, gripping the pistol.

He shrugged. "I make it me business to pick up a bit o' news here and a bit there, for news is money for a fluter like me. And I'd have thought nothin' of it if I hadn't seen this same crippled fella coming out o' your room past midnight."

"And what is that to you?"

"Well, ye never can tell, sir. But if ye have a line on the whereabouts of Jean Le Garde, it'd be a gold piece and more in me pocket, for everybody's interested in the chap."

"I have never set eyes on him."

"Queer, that," said he. "For the road's not that wide from Beauvais to St-Valery that you'd be likely to miss each other."

"You talk too much," I said.

"And you don't talk enough, sir, an' that's the truth of it. Is it asking too much to know if you've seen a missing man?"

I said, getting up, "If I'd seen Le Garde, or whatever his name is, on the St-Valery road, I'd have told the man who was asking for him. I'd not do business with a cowardly Irish fluter who's traveling abroad while his country lies in chains. Now get down that road before I put a bullet in ye."

"You're fine hospitable company, ye heathen!"

"Get going—I'm warning you."

I watched while he mounted the horse and set the little dog on the saddle before him.

Reining in, he said, "Good-by, me son, and right good luck to you, for all yer appalling manners. Aren't ye good for a franc or so to help an Irish fluter on his way?"

"Not a sou," I said, "for the likes of you."

Standing in the quarry entrance, I watched him jogging

down the moonlit road in the direction of the Creton Belle.

There were some queer old people on the road to Paris.

I got into the bedroll then while Mia kept watch, but I did not sleep.

After a bit a twig cracked nearby and I sprang up, the pistol leveled again, and a voice rang out, "Sure to heaven, it's something to have a bad conscience. Good day, Captain Wentworth!"

And he galloped off into the sun.

The Black Midget

The pistol ball ricocheted off the roadside rock beside my head and whined away into the distance, swishing and clattering among the autumn trees. The report echoed in staccato crashes through the forest.

I was off Mia faster than a monkey, pulling her down flat beside me on the rough road. With my pistol leveled over her saddle, I stared down into the valley. Nothing moved in the shimmering heat of late afternoon; faintly I heard the bass lowing of an ox. Crawling to the other side of the road, I stared up at a jutting hill. The day lazed in heat; sheep cried in cracked soprano.

It was impossible to guess where the shot had come from, for the hill was too far for the carry of a pistol. With a tingling scalp, I clambered up, brushing down my clothes, aware that I was again a sitting target for my unseen enemy, and Mia rolled a wary eye at me as if dying to be gone. Once she was on her feet I was astride her and we went like scalded devils down the road to Paris. Behind us billowed the dust of the road to St-Denis; before us rose the spires and turrets of Aubervilliers and Romainville. Soon the roofs of Paris blazed in the September sun.

Men of strange dress were on the streets; women, shawled and starving in their rags of poverty, or daintily stepping under parasols in robes of silk and satin pilfered from the wardrobes of the gentry. A dancing bear was lumbering to the music of a melodeon; a scaffold was being built for an execution in Bastille Square. I trotted Mia slowly among the gay, market crowds. The smell of revolution was still in the air, and news of Bonaparte's victories from the Illyrian Provinces to Hamburg were pouring in weekly. Serfdom and feudalism were on all sides being overthrown, rebellions fanned in every quarter of the world. With the death of the fearful Robespierre a distant memory, Paris danced in her freedom from fear and struck this new-found gaiety on the medal of laughter and bright colors. Yet, there were men who hated this era of joy: men who schemed and planned for the return of the old, hated aristocracy, and such men as these were financed and supported by the government of England.

One of these was Petit Pierre, who, because of his dark countenance and misshaped body, men called the Black Midget.

Passing the stark ruins of the blackened Bastille, I took Mia down the tortuous, narrow Rue de Victoire. Here, under the leaning balconies of a past age of glory, were now growing the slums of the new order of democracy. Past shuttered windows we went, sending mangy cats scuttling off down the cobbled street. A tattered mongrel watched with hopeless eyes as I dismounted and tethered Mia to the broken railings of cellar number sixteen. Taking a deep breath, I went slowly down the broken steps of a mansion that had once housed a silk-clad aristocracy. Before a sagging door I paused and knocked. Instantly it opened, as if someone was expecting me. The bile of fear rose in my throat, but I swallowed it down, saying softly in the darkness of the passage, "I seek Monsieur Petit Pierre."

A voice said, "There is nobody of such a name in this house. Who is visiting?"

"An English officer, Captain Paul Wentworth."

"Wait, if you please." The door closed behind me. I heard echoing footsteps, then a muffled discussion at the end of the passage. In English, a voice whispered, "Enter, Monsieur." A man's face took shape in that dim light, and suddenly he lit a candle, bathing the cellar passage in flickering light. His brutal eyes stared down at me: a giant of a man this, six inches taller than I, his tattered black smock stretched tightly over his wide shoulders. The smell of him crept about and possessed me. "You have papers?" he muttered.

"Yes, I have papers; also a letter from the man of the Creton Belle."

"Give them to me." His hand went out.

"I give the papers only to Monsieur Pierre," I replied.

"I will see that they are delivered. If more is required of you, we will ask it."

I said evenly, "I am an English officer. I have traveled from London with Jean Le Garde. I am responsible only to Monsieur Pierre. Now take me to him, or I will return to London."

The man smiled down, his little black eyes drifting over me in quiet assessment. "The English have spirit still, eh? It is good to have spirit when one is young. But soon, my friend, you might have to account to me. Come!"

I followed him along the passage and up some stairs. There could have been a dungeon beyond this. The nail-studded door rasped in the giant's hand. In French, he said, "He demands to see you, Monsieur; he will accept no other."

I entered a large, dimly lit room. I glanced over my shoulder as the door crashed behind me. The big man was guarding it, feet astride, arms folded, his little eyes glowering in his face.

Before me, perched on a high stool behind a table sat Petit Pierre, the Black Midget.

Never, even in nightmares, have I seen such a man.

He was about sixty years old and dark in the face, but it was more the darkness of evil. Hunched, misshapen, he was perched on the stool rather like a prehistoric bird of prey. He was heavily bearded, and his crinkly black hair flowed to his shoulders. Below the waist his limbs appeared normal, but I saw with a shock that they were the limbs of a child. Before him were documents, ink, and plume; an oil lamp was spluttering on the table, flinging into his face the branding shadows of his pain. He spoke, then, and his voice was beautiful, as if coming from a rent in the shroud of his soul.

"You are Captain Paul Wentworth?" He peered at me over the lamp.

"I am."

"You met our man at the Creton Belle?"

"I did." I laid on the desk the letter this man had given me.

"I will also need your papers and passport, and the letter of introduction from London."

I handed him all the papers I had taken from the dead body of Captain Wentworth. He read with expressionless eyes, muttering, "Jean Le Garde is dead, they tell me."

Sweat was forming on my face. It was the oppressive heat of the room and the strange, faint perfume that emanated from the man before me. I said with an effort, "We —we were ambushed outside St-Valery . . ."

"That is not news, Captain Wentworth—you expected an ambush, did you not? But not outside St-Valery. Did not Jean Le Garde mention this?"

I took a chance. "He said the ambush by the Irish would come south of Beauvais."

"I warned him of where it would come, but he did not listen. So he paid with his life. Now his opinions are not important." He raised his haggard face to mine. "Only the living are important, is that not so, Captain Wentworth?"

To this I did not answer but glanced around the room with a casualness I did not feel. The dwarf read silently, grunting from time to time. I heard myself say, "If there is any doubt as to my identity, Monsieur, perhaps you might care to question me, either on my background in the British army or on my instructions concerning the man Wolfe Tone."

The time for boldness, my father said once, is when the situation begins to slip from your grasp. Petit Pierre grunted in his beard, "There is no need. You are amply vouched for by the English government, and our counteragent at the Creton Belle who interviewed you there is fully satisfied." He rose and, to my astonishment, he was much shorter standing than sitting down. He began to pace the room, his thick fingers, sinewy and black with hair, clasped behind his back. Despite my pity for him, I knew a deep revulsion. He snapped, "Tell me why you have been sent here."

"To assassinate Theobald Wolfe Tone, the Irish leader in the French Directory. To discover the deployment, landing date, and numbers of the French invasion force that is to attempt to drive the British out of Ireland."

"The plan is changed," he replied curtly. "Gascoigne here will kill Wolfe Tone. It is a job for a man, not a stripling officer. From this moment it is your task to bring me the invasion information." He lit a black cheroot, clenching it in his broken teeth. Cocking it up in his bearded face he stared up at me arrogantly, rocking back on his heels. "Now, tell me, young man, how you intend to achieve this."

I replied quickly, "I only obey orders. It is up to you to give me the instructions."

"*Aha!* That is good! You leave the brains to Petit Pierre, eh! Excellent." He waved the cheroot in my face. "It is good to have obedience. Now, then. You are aware that Wolfe Tone's headquarters here is expecting a replacement officer for one killed recently?"

"I was not aware of it."

He spread his hands at me. "How, then, did you expect to enter the service of so astute a man? The Irish in France are not fools, *mon ami*. Neither, come to that, am I!" He laughed harshly, turning to his guard. "What say you, Gascoigne?"

"The master is a genius, Monsieur."

"Aha, a genius! You hear that, English officer? Me, Petit Pierre, I am a genius. Foresight, my friend—foresight is the basis of good spying. The moment I hear that they send for a replacement officer from Ireland, I do two things. First I arrange for such an officer to be sent from England to fill this important post on the Irish staff. Next I capture the replacement officer the United Irishmen sent out from Dublin. *Voilà!* We make what you call a swap. And everybody is happy. You spy for the French and

English allies, the Irish officer goes to the galleys. What you think, eh?"

My tongue was dry in a mouth of dust. I heard myself say, "You—you captured the Irish replacement, Monsieur?"

"*Certainement!* We have him here, eh, Gascoigne?"

"Only this morning we have him here," said the giant.

The dwarf bellowed fierce laughter. "Here he come, as large as life, as you say, all ready to report to the headquarters of Wolfe Tone, and *voilà!* we snatch him from the streets. And he end up here in the dungeon of number sixteen, Rue de Victoire. Is this not clever, Captain Wentworth?"

"It is genius," I whispered. "I trust he was carrying his uniform."

"We do not even have to alter his uniform; it will fit you like a glove. His passport, his papers, and his name you will take—Lieutenant Michael Hearne. By first light tomorrow you go to St-Denis, the headquarters of Wolfe Tone . . ."

"Lieutenant Michael Hearne," I said softly.

"It is an excellent Irish name for you, eh? It drips off the tongue." The midget jerked his thumb at the floor. "And at dawn next Thursday, this Irish fool, he go another way—to the office of the recruiter-general of Spanish navy. Within a week he will be chained to an oar and under the whip off Cádiz." His expression changed from joy to ferocity as he stared up at me. "Where all such fools end when they pit their wits against the genius, Petit Pierre."

"It is no more than they deserve," I said.

"No more, Monsieur, no less. Remember this when you spy for me. You want to see this Irish fool whose place you take?"

"It is of no importance," I muttered, sick at heart.

"Ah, but it is. His manner to watch, his speech you can hear. Gascoigne here will beat him again, and perhaps he will speak. But he do not speak so far, except to call to Ireland. Such is his stupidity, when he is bound for the galleys of Spain!"

I clenched my hands until the nails bit deep into my palms as I followed them downstairs to the place of his captivity. We came to a door. Gascoigne fumbled with a key in the dim light and swung the door open.

A young man, naked to the waist, was lying face down on the earth floor. I could see the blood upon his face when he raised himself on an elbow, blinking at the candle in Gascoigne's hand. And I saw beyond him a tiny window near the ceiling, and through this window the other side of the Rue de Victoire. September flowers were growing in profusion there, splashing red and gold over a rotting door.

Pierre cried, "We bring you a visitor, Irish fool! It is the English officer who will take your post in the Irish headquarters. You speak to him, eh, so he can hear your voice?"

The young man rose weakly to his feet. Gascoigne held the candle higher so the flame lit his face. I nearly gasped with surprise. The man standing before me was the Irish beggar from the Creton Belle.

He said, gripping his hands, "So it was you after all. My

God, I shouldn't have missed you in that ambush! You're the dregs of manhood, you're not fit to live!"

"English officer and Irish fool—you meet before, eh?"

I said, "He suspected who I was, and tried to ambush me just outside Paris."

"Captain in the English army, eh?" breathed the patriot. "I wonder how far you'll get with a man like Wolfe Tone?"

"Far enough, you will see," I said.

"But he will not see," cried Pierre. "Soon he will be in the galleys, and you eating his dinner in the Irish headquarters!" And he shouted with laughter, stamping about.

In that laughter the young patriot moved. With astonishing speed, he launched himself at me, and his fist caught me square. Staggering back, I fell. Blood trickled from my split lip, dropping in widening stains on my shirt. Instantly Gascoigne leaped over me, clubbing the patriot down. Petit Pierre was bending over him now, shrieking insults into his face as I staggered to my feet.

"Leave him, Monsieur, he is not worth it," I said. "He will get worse off Cádiz than anything Gascoigne could hand him now. Come, sir, come!" I dragged at Pierre. "Let us away to the business at hand—I say leave him."

And in the instant before the guard slammed and locked the dungeon door, I saw the little window again, and beyond it, the red and gold flowers on the Rue de Victoire.

Pierre said, "Our counteragent at the Creton Belle at first suspected you. Luckily for us he picked the guilty one, which was clever. For it is not every replacement in Wolfe Tone's headquarters who enters France with a dog and a flute. You give us credit for first-rate espionage, Captain?"

"I give you credit, Monsieur Pierre," I replied.

But I was not really listening to him. With my handkerchief stanching the blood from my mouth, I was giving a silent prayer for the young patriot.

The Irish Wolf

Before I left the cellar of Petit Pierre next morning, I wrote on a scrap of paper a single word: *Courage.*

All eyes turned to me as I cantered down the Rue de Victoire on that bright September morning, for it is not every day of the week that Paris sees a lieutenant in the blue of the United Irishmen, and the uniform of Michael Hearne suited me fine. More than one winsome wench in a bodice of lace and a blood-red petticoat smoothed back her hair for a better look, for there's no doubt about uniforms putting the shivers in the women. Even Mia once or twice glanced over her mane at me, wondering if she had the right fella aboard. Through the market-square crowd we went, with the Parisians calling good morning, the men doffing their cockade hats of revolution blue, the ladies dropping a curtsey to a young foreign officer.

At the end of the street I clattered Mia about and we went back again until we reached the red and gold flowers of the house façade. I immediately found the tiny window of the patriot's cell, set in a crack of the pavement. Dismounting, I knelt. Rolling the precious message around a stone, I dropped it down the little aperture. Then, with forced casualness, I remounted Mia and trotted her along the cobbles toward St-Denis.

I could not do otherwise. In less than a week Michael Hearne would be chained to a galley oar, and I could not leave him without a single hope of life, though my father would have flayed me alive for taking such a risk at such a time.

I overtook the mail coach as it rumbled north from the center of Paris, and fine it looked indeed, with four great horses galloping and the coach swaying, and I loved the clattering commotion of it all.

The sun was climbing its ladder of gold as I reined Mia in and trotted into St-Denis.

I did not know that Wolfe Tone, with his usual scrupulous attention to detail, always insisted on personally receiving even the most junior officer replacement. Entering the wide-lawned headquarters of the Irish army in Paris, I had little opportunity to appreciate the great rambling mansion, the gabled and turreted nerve center of the coming invasion of my country. Challenged immediately by the Irish sentry, I was escorted to the guard room. There a French major received me with a cold stare.

"Lieutenant Michael Hearne."

"Yes, sir." I stood at attention before him.

"You are late."

"I was delayed . . ."

"You are over twenty-four hours late. Why is this so?" He wore the uniform of the brilliant *cuirassieurs*, the death-or-glory horsemen of the vanguard of Bonaparte. I did not reply and his cold, merciless eyes snapped up at me. "The colonel will want to know why you are late reporting."

One thing was already clear. Even Wolfe Tone's closest officer did not know my true identity. If this was so then doubtless the great man himself believed it to be Lieutenant Michael Hearne reporting. The major rose from his desk. "Come this way," he snapped.

As I followed him down a corridor I noticed Mia being led away for stabling and fodder across the square. The major threw open an ornate door.

"*Entrez*, André!" called a voice, and the major saluted, closing the door behind me. I was standing in a great vaulted room. On the sea of crimson carpet before me was a mahogany desk, and at it was seated a colonel of the French army of Napoleon, wearing a uniform of dazzling blue. On his left breast was a square of bright green and on this was embroidered a shamrock. He was middle-aged and of average build. Indeed, but for the uniform with its gold epaulets and braid, he could have been mistaken for the adjutant, except for his eyes.

I knew at once that this was Wolfe Tone. It was his eyes. Never have I seen such eyes: they met mine and held me rooted at the door. And then, as if remembering the effect, he smiled and rose, hand out.

"Lieutenant Hearne, Dublin Militia?"

Stiff to attention, I gripped his hand. Again, those eyes, of a man of destiny. They seemed to search my soul.

I said, softly, "No, sir. I am not Lieutenant Hearne. I am John Regan, sent by Caine Adams of the Wexford United Irishmen."

He smiled brilliantly. "This is not so, Regan. Your name is Michael Hearne. Your rank is lieutenant in the Dublin Militia. Is that quite clear?"

I returned his smile. "Yes, sir."

He added, sitting down, "Never for a moment forget this. Tell me, how fares Michael Hearne?"

"You—you know of this, sir?"

"Of course. When are they taking him from the Rue de Victoire?"

"At dawn next Thursday, sir." I stared at him. "But how—how could you possibly know?"

"Do not concern yourself with this. Suffice it to say that I do. Accept my regrets on the death of Patrick Hays, your friend. We have lost Caine Adams too, did you know this?"

I bowed my head. "This I was told by Jean Le Garde."

He nodded. "Who also died, with the English Captain Wentworth." He rose and walked to the great window behind him and stood with his back to me, in outline against an avenue of giant oaks and a sky of cobalt blue. Like a god he looked, standing there; upon his shoulders lay the fate of Ireland. He continued, "It was a pity that Wentworth had to die. He was a good officer, if an enemy.

Jean Le Garde came from a very different bed, one of high aristocracy, but he was an evil man." Turning, he said with a smile, "It is poetic retribution that Le Garde should die. He was the man who ambushed and shot your father—did you know this?"

I knew only that my father, on an earlier mission, had been shot in the back on the road to Milford.

Wolfe Tone added, "A word of warning, Regan, before I forget this. You crossed Captain Wentworth with the rapier, but did you realize his skill? He was senior instructor in the London School of the Sword and would certainly have killed you had not Jean Le Garde shot him accidentally. The rapier is now old-fashioned, young man —stick to the pistol. In this business we take no gallant chances."

It was astonishing to me that he knew these facts, and in such detail, for nobody saw Wentworth die except Jean Le Garde and the coachman. Perhaps he apprehended this astonishment, for he added, "But we are concerned with the present, not with the past, Regan. Your dangers are just beginning, do you realize this?" He added, "There are special dangers for double agents."

"Yes, sir."

"I would have it no different for us, for we are Irishmen. According to my reports, you have obtained the complete confidence of Pierre and the French Committee. Nurture this, maintain this, or you are lost. It is necessary that they be fed incorrect information of our plans and movements. You know the detailed information?"

"I do, sir. Caine Adams arranged that Patrick Hays and I be briefed by the Rebel Committee in Wexford before we set sail with him and Marcel Robet . . ."

His eyes were twinkling as he sat down. "Kindly repeat it," he said.

I took a breath. "The number sailing will be thirty thousand officers and men. There will be three ships of the line and fifty frigates. The expedition will be commanded by Commodore Rochelle; you will be aboard the *Expedite*. The invasion force will leave Cherbourg on the twenty-eighth of this month. The landing will be made on the Irish coast at Galway."

Wolfe Tone smiled and lowered his head, whispering, "I have great friends indeed in this lonely exile from my country. Who told you this, you say?"

"The Rebel Committee of Wexford, sir, but the brief came from Caine Adams."

"Rest his soul, Ireland will miss him," came the reply. "You realize, of course, that the information is totally wrong?"

I rose slowly, staring down at him, and he said, "Totally wrong, Regan. Incorrect plans were given to you in case somebody forced them from your lips. But they are good enough for Pierre and the French spy committee. Tonight you will return to the Rue de Victoire and inform him of these fictitious facts. By this evening I will have them written out on what purports to be a secret document. The true information I will give you in due course, after you return."

I said, "Is this not very early, sir? How could I possibly obtain such secret information in so short a time?"

"Do as you are told, Regan, and leave the thinking to me." Wolfe Tone looked up, his eyes unmoving on mine.

"And—and Michael Hearne, sir?"

"What of him?"

"He languishes in a cellar dungeon. His treatment is brutal. He has been a pawn in the game . . ."

"We are all pawns in the game of liberating our country, Regan. What is your life, or Lieutenant Hearne's —what is my life, considering the stakes for which we fight? Would Caine Adams have counted the cost, or Father Murphy, or my gallant comrades Bagenal Harvey, Keugh, Colclough, and a thousand others? Your father died the death of a hero, Regan. Would he have complained?"

I replied, "With respect, sir, it is useless to lose a life we could save. Two men—just two men to aid me—and I would bring him here tonight!"

"Oho!" He leaned back in his chair and clasped his hands with a new regard. "The son has the same bright fever of the father, I see." Then his expression changed. "But the son, like the father, will do as he is told. Michael Hearne, in the cause of his country, will go to the Spanish galleys." He emptied his hands at me with a gesture of conciliation. "Later, if we are successful, I will talk to the French admirals and we will do what we can to retrieve him. But to shift a finger to free him now would raise the suspicions of the French Committee and Pierre. The wrong information *must* be sent to London. I will not jeopardize the lives of thousands to save the life of one, do you hear me?"

I stood rigidly to attention. "I do, sir."

He smiled and adopted a broad Irish brogue. "Right, then— away wi' ye and report to the adjutant major. Be ready to return to the Rue de Victoire by dusk tonight."

At the door I said, "Your life, too, sir, is at stake. Pierre has commanded your assassination. There is a man named Gascoigne, a giant from Grenoble . . ."

He rubbed his chin, smiling. "The big Gascoigne, eh? Tell him, John Regan, that I will be delighted to receive him. He will not be the first to attempt it, neither will he be the last."

Standing to attention, I saluted Theobald Wolfe Tone.

If a man has to die, let it be in such company.

The Lifting of the Mask

At dusk that evening I rode Mia down the Rue de Victoire and saw the great column that marked the spot of the ignoble prison, the Bastille. It was an evening of strange quiet, as if the populace, in a sudden memory of the Reign of Terror, had crept behind the latticed windows, there to rock themselves and moan at the thought.

And in the clatter of Mia's hoofs I saw, in my mind's eyes, a transformation in the streets. I saw through the intervening years the bloody barricades, the scythe-armed tattered mob of the gutter slums of Paris, the cackling, red-eyed market women and the fisherwomen of the fleets, who knitted and patched within reach of the blade of *Madame Guillotine*. The crackle of musketry I heard, the boom of cannon, and the shrieking of prisoners. I saw, too, the dignity of a dissolute gentry, standing in the rumbling tumbrils amid the frenzied, blood-stained mobs. The flash of satin and lace I saw, and the fluttering of rags. And I thought, as I rode along the cobbles of this foreign city, of my Wexford that had known a fate no less horrible.

In my ears I still heard the screaming of the women burning in the barn of Scullabogue; I saw the hideous massacres of New Ross and Vinegar Hill; I remembered the shame of the holocaust at Wexford Bridge. I saw in my memory the noble dignity of the patriot Keugh as he faced the rope on Wexford Bridge; heard again the pleas of the prisoners dragged from Three Rocks for slaughter; and saw, through my tears, Cornelius Grogan, the innocent patriarch with white hair to his shoulders, hobbling to the scaffold on crutches. Along the roads of Ireland still lay the stripped and mutilated bodies of my people, innocent victims of the lust for revenge of the red-breasted English soldiery and the vicious German mercenaries, who were paid in English money for their atrocities on the helpless body of my country.

Most of my heroes were gone now, my idols shattered into dust. The great Bagenal Harvey was dead, hanged like a felon. Father John Murphy, the hero of Boolavogue and Enniscorthy, kissed the soil of his land before he raised his eyes to the noose. Here, in this Paris of rebellion, I seemed to see them all again, and my scalp was crawling as I reached the cell window of Michael Hearne on the Rue de Victoire.

A low whining came from the pavement, and I pulled Mia up, searching the shadows.

The little dancing dog of Michael Hearne was lying there, its nose buried in its outstretched paws, weeping for its master. I spurred Mia on, for in the business of life or death there is no time for weeping dogs. But deep within me, I wept at the sight of such undying love.

The cellar door of Petit Pierre was opened to my knock; by Pierre, to my surprise.

"Ah, my fine friend, you are back so early?"

I followed him to his room; there was no sign of the giant Gascoigne. The midget sat on his high stool and rubbed his hands together. "So soon you have information for me?"

"I have some, Monsieur," I replied.

"Name it."

I said, sitting down, "Were you aware that I am personal assistant to Wolfe Tone? This was the appointment of Michael Hearne."

"I was not aware. But this is excellent! In this position of trust you will be able to see all secret documents!"

"I have already seen some; the safe is in my keeping." I took from my pocket the invasion disposition Wolfe Tone had given to me and tossed it on the table before Pierre. He snatched it up, reading voraciously. I watched him. His eyes began to open wide beneath his shaggy brows, and he whispered, *"Mon Dieu!* It is here—the whole disposition! Thirty thousand men, three battleships, and fifty frigates. But wait!" He climbed down off his stool, trembling with excitement. "The twenty-eighth of this month!" His fist crashed down on the table. "From Cherbourg under Colar Rochelle. I knew it, I *knew* it!" Rushing past me, he paused only to clap me on the back and I stiffened with disgust. Running to the door, he flung it open, shouting, "Gascoigne, Gascoigne! Come, come!" He danced about. "Oh, I am delighted!"

I sat in the chair, my hand gripping my rapier, and as Gascoigne came, flushed and breathless, Petit Pierre cried up at him, "Quick, quick, bring the messenger, bring him!"

Gascoigne dashed away and Pierre ran back to the table. Seizing an envelope, he wrote swiftly with a plume, attached his message to the disposition, and sealed it. In seconds a messenger appeared.

The midget thrust the envelope into his hands, crying, "Your life is forfeit—away to London! Change horses at the Creton Belle. Go straight to the French Committee to Monsieur Carvil. Deliver this instantly, there is not a moment to lose!"

Returning to the table, Pierre poured a volume of congratulations over me. As I listened to the messenger galloping away, he said, "It is as I told London—despite them all, I insisted it would be Rochelle from Cherbourg. But time is short . . ." Tense, he began to tremble.

"An able commodore, according to Tone," I interjected.

Pierre's eyes were shining with jubilation. "He received you so soon?" He added, "Is it not astonishing he received you so soon!"

"He personally receives all his officers, however junior. He has hundreds about him, United Irish and French, yet he knows every one of them by name." At this point I rose. "But this, to my mind, is his sole quality. He is a man of gentry arrogance and intolerance!"

Pierre smiled benignly, his fingers tented before his face. "And you have no liking for this gentility?"

"It is not gentility!" I swung to him. "It is profound bad manners!"

With my face turned away from him I allowed myself a little silent stupefaction, for it appeared to me that I was acting well, and I was normally an appalling actor. In the little nativity plays of the schools of Wexford they always relegated me to a very minor role, like holding the train of one of the Three Kings. Apparently I was improving, for the midget said, "You dislike Wolfe Tone?"

I turned to face him. "Yes, and I dislike your assassin. Gascoigne is a lumbering fool, and he will make a mess of the killing. I will be with Tone twenty-four hours a day—"

He interjected, suavely, "Perhaps you are too young, too rash for such a job, *mon ami*."

I said, "I am neither. But I am ambitious. My name will stand high in the esteem of the English army if I execute Wolfe Tone." My voice rose. "He is an enemy of the British Empire, he is the wolf that tears at the coat of Royal France!"

"Ambition can be a hangman, Monsieur," he said softly.

"That is the chance I take. Send Gascoigne back to the peasant village to which he belongs. Allow me to serve your beloved France!"

At this he rose again, strutting about me with a peacock approbation, and said, "For what you have brought me, I grant this wish. Bring me the head of Theobald Wolfe Tone and Royal France will reward you with privilege and honor!" In a sudden passion he cried, "New France will grow from the ashes of the peasant rebellion! New thrones will rise, new kings will flourish in the empire of the east. And we will sweep this rebellious rubbish from our doors and raise a new Bastille and new guillotines for the necks of the street-gutter traitors. *Vive la France!*"

"You will give me this task—you will grant this to me?" I begged, my hands out to him. Outwardly trembling with excitement, I was sick within at the thought of a man like Wolfe Tone in the hands of a beast like Gascoigne.

"It is little enough to ask, my son. Come."

We had hardly turned for the door when Gascoigne knocked.

"*Entrez, entrez!*" cried Pierre, impatiently.

The door came open. The giant stood there, fumbling with his hands.

"Well, what is it?" demanded Pierre.

"Monsieur Marcel Robet asks to see you," said the man.

Ice formed between my brain and my skull. Quickly I cried, "But I demand your attention first, Pierre. If I go now . . ." I strode toward the door, then backed away as Marcel Robet entered. No longer was he a humble fishing-boat skipper. Handsome he looked in his aristocratic clothes, this man who had drowned Patrick, my friend, and murdered Caine Adams. The pistol in his hand was steady.

"You are staying here, John Regan," he said.

Gascoigne closed the door behind him, grinning. The eyes of Petit Pierre were like coals of fire in his monstrous face.

This is how wars are lost. I had forgotten the existence of Marcel Robet.

Recovering himself, Pierre shouted, "Do you know who this young man is, Robet?"

"I do. But you do not, Pierre. I landed two Irish spies at St-Valery several days ago. Although I landed them in impossible water, only one of them drowned. This one survived, I find. The man I employed to signal with a lantern saw him come ashore, and I have only just learned it."

"You fool, Robet!" shouted Pierre in gusty laughter. "This is Captain Wentworth from London—even our man at the Creton Belle has accepted him!"

"The only fool here is you, Pierre. Wentworth was killed. This man is impersonating him."

Disbelief was still written on the midget's face, and Gascoigne said, "He has made a fool of me, too, master. This note I find in the hand of Lieutenant Hearne, the prisoner—only this minute I find it, and nobody but this one knows he is here."

Pierre's face changed as he took the note, then he said,

"Courage, eh? You write this, my friend? A double agent, are you? If this is true you will need all the courage you have got, Monsieur." Motionless, he glared up at me.

Marcel Robet turned away and said, "Nothing is lost, Pierre. But you can thank your stars I identified him before he gave you fictitious news to send away to London —that would be a pretty case to answer."

I said, smiling, "But you have arrived too late, Robet."

Realization struck the midget and he swung on his heel, shouting, "The disposition, the disposition! Stop the messenger, stop the messenger!"

"But he has already left, and at speed, Monsieur!" cried Gascoigne as he approached me. I hooked him hard, but it was like striking rock. I remember nothing after he beat me to my knees.

To the Galleys

"Go and eat, go and eat, my foolish little Pepi," said Mike
Hearne at the cell window. For in the little niche of stone
two small eyes were shining. Never have I heard a little
dog cry as Pepi cried for Mike Hearne, her master.

I raised myself on the straw pallet in a corner of the
dungeon and felt my battered face.

"He's got a punch on him like a Tipperary mule, that
big Gascoigne," said Mike over his shoulder. "How's your
jaw?"

I felt it, wagging it sideways. "I reckon he hit me with a
seven-pound hammer," I said, sitting upright.

"As long as ye can eat wi' it," said Mike. "The big
thing is to be able to eat wi' it."

"There's no point in eating for the place we're going," I
said. "The sooner you're out of it, the better."

"Och, not at all," came the answer. "While there's life,
there's hope—you told me that yourself an hour back."

"That was an hour back. I'm changing me mind from
minute to minute," I said.

"Would a tune on the flute mend ye?" asked Mike. "For you're looking miserable to death."

Squatting before me, he fished out his flute. Boyish and handsome he looked, his bruised face square and strong, and he said, "The last time I played this thing the big fella came in and handed me a hammering. But maybe that was because I gave him Killarney. We'll try him with a Wexford song of home." Turning up his face he shouted at the ceiling, "D'ye hear that, Pepi? It's ye favorite comin' up!"

And so he played for me. With renewed courage, for Gascoigne had beaten me badly, I rose, staring up at the window ten feet above. High, shrill, and pretty he played that flute.

"Dear God," I whispered.

"What's up, John?" asked Mike.

"She's dancing—look!" I pointed up at the slit of light. "The wee girl's dancing!"

Mike Hearne swallowed hard. "The dog has no brain," said he. "Tell her not to be daft."

"What do ye think they have in store for us?" Mike asked late that night.

"Starve us to death, more than likely," I replied.

For three days I had been in the cell, Mike nearly five. But Gascoigne had brought us only scraps of food, flung in like a man feeding a dog. And we might have died of thirst had it not rained. Water trickled down from the crack in the pavement and we caught it in our hands, drinking greedily.

Mike said, "I doubt it. If little Pierre can get fifty francs apiece from the Spanish galleys, I can't see him letting us starve."

"Listen," I whispered. "Somebody's coming."

Faintly, too, on the road overhead, came the unmistakable clatter of a coach. Heavy footsteps echoed in the passage beyond the door. Gascoigne entered, followed by Marcel Robet, who held a pistol.

"Good evening, Messieurs!" greeted the giant. "The compliments of Petit Pierre himself. You are ready for the galleys?"

"Tie their hands quickly, and do not waste time, you fool!" muttered Robet. "It is a mistake, I say—Pierre is money-mad. If I had my way I would slit their throats."

"But a hundred francs is not to be sneezed at, Marcel!"

"Then let Pierre get them to the coast. I tell you, it is dangerous!"

"Oh, no, my friend. Pierre is clever—he only does the spending." Gascoigne heaved at Mike's hands, cruelly tightening the knot. Roped together, with our arms pinioned, they took us down the passage and through the street door. There was no sign of Pepi in the Rue de Victoire. She either was dead or had gone, said Mike.

They thrust us into the coach, with Marcel Robet on one side of us, Gascoigne on the other. We did not speak as we galloped through Bastille and took north along the road to Chantilly.

"Calais, Messieurs!" shouted Robet above the clattering wheels. "At Calais is the office of the recruiter-general of the Spanish navy. And he does not like Irishmen."

"There you will be fettered, my good friends," added Gascoigne.

I lowered my head, thankful for the darkness. The rushing blackness of the autumn hedgerows beat about us, but I did not smell their sweetness. I smelled, instead, the indescribable stink that was the hallmark of the filthy Spanish galleys and felt the lash of the overseer's whip. In my hands I gripped the shining, sweat-stained oar and saw the incinerating brilliance of the Bay of Setúbal.

"At Calais you will be blinded, you know this?" asked Gascoigne, grinning.

Robet said, "It is the recommendation of Petit Pierre. The recruiter will be advised that you are dangerous men —it is safer that you be blinded."

I shut my eyes, a revulsion growing within me at the inhumanity of men.

And then Mike said suddenly, "Go to the devil, Robet. You know, John, I've been thinking. I reckon somebody pinched my little Pepi, for she wouldn't have left that window unless I'd driven her off."

"Silence! You do not speak!" shouted Robet harshly.

And the brutal galley shout of the Spanish overseer beat in my brain. I heard the rhythmic booming of the drum and saw the sunburned back of the rower in front of me. I heard the overseer's command as he bawled the time: *Seis, siete, ocho! Seis, siete, ocho! Seis, siete, ocho!*

"Oh, Lady of Chantilly!" I whispered.

The coach rumbled on through the moonlight. In the middle of Chantilly we slowed to a walk, and Gascoigne put his head out of the window.

"What is happening, coachman?" he demanded.

Mike said, "If the pair of you had ever been to church, you'd know. It is the midnight celebration of Our Lady of the Flowers."

"The what?" rumbled Gascoigne beside me.

"The annual carnival," I said. "The Lady of the Flowers is the Mother of Jesus, or perhaps you've never heard of her."

The coach plodded on through the outskirts of the town, and I thought of the vagabond François Malon, who lived here, and how he had lifted me of ten gold sovereigns. This was the devil-may-care town of France, a place of duels and high honor—a strange combination of reckless daring and piety. My father always said that before he drew a rapier in France, he first inquired if his opponent was raised in Chantilly, since not only would he be an expert swordsman but a devout man, and God would surely be on his side in the quarrel.

A tumult of voices grew about us as we clattered along the narrow, cobbled streets, and the red light of bonfires began to dance dervishes on the coach windows. Distantly came the strains of music, the glorious harmony of peasant voices raised in the incantations of a midnight mass.

Mike turned his face and lifted an eyebrow at me and I nodded. A midnight procession might be the very thing we needed. Slower, slower we went, and people began to gather about us. Street bonfires flashed red on the lace bodices of the women and the satin sheen of breeches as men danced their wives and sweethearts in little rings. Bands were playing, old crones chattering, children shrieking with delight. And in the middle of the gaiety the towering effigies of the saints swayed and turned. All was love and beauty, and I thought it inconceivable that cruelty could exist amid such benevolence. We in that coach seemed a creeping stain on the tapestry of God. Then, suddenly, the coach ground shrilly to a halt, the door was flung open, and a young girl peered in. All sparkling with excitement was she, with her hair flying free to her waist, and around her forehead was a ring of flowers. Her hands begged at us, and she cried, "Oh, strangers in Chantilly, come, join in the dancing!" And she showered us with a basket of blossoms.

"Away, away!" cried Robet in a panic, concealing us with his body.

"Then let the young men come, sir, do not be perverse!"

"I am an extremely good dancer!" yelled Mike, and Gascoigne slammed the coach door and clapped his hand over his mouth, but the door came open again and more maidens pushed in, shrieking with laughter and pelting us with flowers.

"Come, let them dance, old gentleman. It is for the Lady of Chantilly—do not be mean!" One begged prettily, eyes closed, hands together in prayer.

"In honor to her, Our Lady! Come, Monsieur, come!"

In a sudden rage Gascoigne leaped up, slammed the door shut, pushed the girls away, and yelled, banging the window, "Driver, driver! Whip up the horses! Ten francs extra if you get us out of Chantilly!"

"Now's our chance!" muttered Mike into my ear.

"No, man—wait, wait!" I said.

Turning, Robet struck me a vicious blow across the mouth. "*Allons*, driver! Gallop, gallop!"

But it was useless. In a gay, festive mood, the crowd surged more thickly about us, and the horses reared and then quieted as the young men took their bridles and led them into the procession. And the moment we were tethered in the thick of it, the doors of the coach came open on either side. The music died to a whisper. The people were hushed, peering in, staring at our bonds.

A man cried, "Are these criminals, Monsieur?" He glared up into Robet's face.

"A thief and a murderer, sir—we are carrying them to Beauvais and the Hall of Justice!" rumbled Gascoigne.

I said, "Neither a thief nor a murderer, sir. We are Irish officers being sent to the galleys—captured in our service to Ireland and France. Look, see my uniform. Have you seen such a uniform?"

"To the galleys?" cried a matron. "Whatever their crime, whoever they are—must they stain the path of Our Lady of Chantilly?"

"It is a scandal!"

"An affront!"

"An insult to Our Lady!"

They whispered among themselves. Ten deep, they peered at us in the light of the bonfires, and I noticed for the first time that armed men were closing in about us. Gascoigne saw them, too, and licked his thick lips. With their hands on their sword hilts, they came slowly, working their way through the crowd.

Then one, taller and older than the rest, put his elbow on the window and smiled up.

"And what are you going to do now, Marcel Robet?"

I stared at this man. Then jubilation grew within me, for I knew that we were free.

I was with him again, feeling the prick of his rapier as I knelt before the forest statue of the Mother of God. I was with him again in the forest clearing outside St-Valery, when he had saved me from Jean Le Garde's evil coachman.

"François Malon!" I breathed.

But he did not appear to hear me, for he said to Robet, "It is a very peaceful ambush, you must agree, Marcel Robet? Surely it is better to be bombarded with September roses than musket balls? And if the mayor had his way he'd cut you limb from limb for interrupting the procession of Our Lady of Chantilly."

"You will pay for this with your life, Malon!" breathed Robet.

"This you have been promising me for the nine years since the revolution began, Monsieur." He turned to me, smiling. "Regan, my master in St-Denis commands that I tell you this: the Rue de Victoire is under police guard and the man Pierre has been taken. Further, my master is sailing in good company within the next twenty-four hours, and the place of his departure will be made known to you when you report to the military at St-Denis. Does this make sense to you, sir?"

"Yes, indeed!" I cried, turning as he cut my bonds.

"Then listen again. Now that I find you alive, your fine big mare, which I stole from the railings of the Rue de Victoire three days ago, must be returned to you—a fact which I regret. You will find her tethered to the stocks of the Chapel of St. John on the other side of the square." He pointed. "When next you are in trouble, for this is becoming a habit, do not hesitate to call upon the services of François Malon."

"And the ten gold pieces you stole from me at St-Valery, sir?" I asked, opening my hand.

"*Mon Dieu,* you Irish drive a hard bargain!" He dropped the purse into my hand.

"For I suspect that our master has paid you well enough, Monsieur. Do we not share the same master in St-Denis?"

At this he straightened to attention and the smile left his face. "Next to Bonaparte, I serve him—the same master as you."

"Colonel Tone, of your glorious army?"

He bowed low to me. "The Irish wolf, the ally of France!"

Leaping from the coach, Mike and I pushed a path through the milling procession, looking back but once among the cheering girls to see Malon and his men leading Marcel Robet and the big Gascoigne away, tied by the same bonds they had used on us.

"You can guess where they're bound!" shouted Mike.

"They'll be lucky to see the guard room in St-Denis," I cried.

"More likely the recruiter-general of the galleys in Calais, if I know that rogue Malon! Fifty francs apiece —that's roughly five gold pieces." He added, shouting excitedly, "Look, there's your horse!"

"And somebody else," I said softly.

For sitting on Mia's saddle in the light of the bonfires was Mike's little Pepi. Seeing Mike, she began to tremble, little cries of joy coming from her throat.

"Malon will not be sending those two to the galleys," I said. "A man who will risk his life for a dog would never do that to a human being."

I turned away while Mike greeted her.

"Hey, up, you!" I cried to Mia. "You're two up now, until we reach St-Denis!"

With the two of us jammed in a stirrup apiece, we galloped away to the south over the flower-strewn square of Our Lady of Chantilly.

"Ireland!" shouted Mike.

"Ireland, *Ireland!*" I cried in the red light of the flares.

A Cunning Foe

We sailed from France on the twentieth day of September, 1798. By the light of a big French moon, we sailed from the Bay de Camaret, Brest, with three thousand men, one ship of the line, and eight frigates loaded to the gunwales with arms for my people. Under the command of General Hardy and Commodore Bompart, we sailed, with Mike and I aboard the *Hoche*, the ship that also carried the hope of Ireland—Colonel Wolfe Tone.

There were the frigates *Loire*, *Résolue*, *Bellone*, *Embuscade*, *Coquille*, and *Romaine*, with the *Sémillante* and *Immortalité* in the vanguard and the schooner *Biche* at stern. And Bompart took us in a big sweep westward, then northeast to avoid the British fleet which was prowling the sea. We were sailing under every stitch of canvas for Loch Swilly at the top of Ireland in County Donegal.

I came up from below decks after seeing to Mia and joined Mike at the rail of the great ship, and the Bay of Biscay was up to her usual tricks, with white-foamed rollers belting westward in challenge to the great, gray Atlantic.

"Is it true he's making for Loch Swilly?" Mike wiped water from his face and pulled his oilskins closer about him, for there was a nip of ice in the wind, despite the month.

"Och, you know Wolfe Tone. He's likely to tell us one thing and then do another," I replied. "Whee jakes! The little *Biche* is taking it bad, can you see?" I pointed.

Two miles astern the little schooner was up to her ears in it, plunging deep and coming up streaming foam. And although the great seventy-four-gun *Hoche* was ten times her size, she, too, began a handy roll, with occasional pitching and tossing that had us clinging to the rail, and sea spray beating in thundering crashes along her bulwarks and rigging.

"According to the bos'n there's bad weather coming up," cried Mike above the wind. "There's wee Pepi sick in me hammock and we've hardly even started."

We walked the pitching deck, our eyes feasting on the thunderous horizon northeast, where lay the shores of Ireland. Young French officers, the cream of the infantry, strolled the decks with the apparent unconcern of their military upbringing. These youngsters, many of them the snuff-taking fops of the Paris salons, their periwigs and gilt making them walking peacocks, were the men who later commanded the bloodstained batteries at Waterloo. These were the heroes of the New France, whose ferocity in battle flung out the boundaries of Napoleon's French empire. Now they were sailing to a foreign land to raise a new revolution—to command, in a foreign tongue, the rebel rabble of the Irish towns and cities.

"Some dandies, eh?" whispered Mike, as we passed them.

"Mention it to them if you want a duel on your hands," I said.

I looked at my new friend. Like granite in strength and purpose he stood, braced to the gale, staring out toward Ireland. He looked resplendent in his uniform, newly appointed to his original post as aide-de-camp to Colonel Tone, while I had been granted the temporary rank of junior lieutenant.

"Glass is droppin', gentlemen," said a sailor, in passing. "Big winds comin' up, beggin' ye pardons, sirs." He was an officer's servant, the only other Irishman aboard.

"We're still heading west?" I asked.

"Just settling down to a northeast tack, sir," cried he, and his tarred pigtail was as straight as a spar in the wind tearing in from the Atlantic. As he braced his legs to the buck and roll of her, waves thundered over the bow and wallowed in foaming hisses down the scuppers. He wiped rain from his face. "Can't get the shelter o' Cape Clear soon enough, if you're askin' me, sir."

"Monsieur!" cried a young French officer beside me. "My apologies, but is the weather always as bad as this near Ireland?"

"You don't know what ye got coming, sir!" cried our sailor gaily.

"Then I will ask my commodore to take me back to France. For I would rather rot on the plains of Kiev than come on a sea voyage with this mad Wolfe Tone!"

"Goin' to get worse before it gets better, sir," cried the sailor.

The bosun staggered past then, crying, "Furl tops'ls. Monkeys aloft. Tops'ls furled and tighten mainmast stays. Aloft, men, aloft!" His hoarse voice bellowed along the decks and the wind snatched it, merging it in the thunder. The mainsheets volleyed, the sheets cracked like pistol shots to the heeling rush of the wind. Rain lashed the top-works and streamed down the glass. I saw Commodore Bompart, the brilliant French seaman who had fought under General Hoche and was now commanding the third French expedition to my country. Wolfe Tone joined him at the rail; their faces, I noticed, were grave. Seeing us, Tone gestured peremptorily. Mike ran, standing to attention before him. Bompart spoke urgently, and Mike saluted. Returning to me, he said, "All officers to the commodore's cabin—you take larboard, I will take starboard. And rip them out o' their hammocks—there must be dozens snoring below."

A few minutes later French naval and army officers were crammed together in the cabin. With Wolfe Tone sitting beside him, Bompart raised a grave face and said, "You should know, gentlemen, that bad weather is coming up, and it is not without its dangers. More, before leaving France I was informed that nothing has been heard of the Napper Tandy expedition which sailed two weeks ago, and it is known that the powerful British squadron of Sir John Borlase Warren is cruising in the vicinity of the Mullet peninsula and Aran Island. . . ." He glanced slowly around the room, and to my embarrassment, his eyes paused on me. Smiling, he added, "On the other hand, gentlemen, we have been afforded good intelligence. A false report of our dispositions, strength, and time of departure is already on its way to the English government in London. According to this report we are ten times our number, six times our strength in fighting ships, and we are due to leave Cherbourg eight days from now."

Wolfe Tone chuckled, lighting his pipe. Laughter spread gustily around the heaving cabin. The commodore went on, "But I am instructed by the naval authorities to inform you of the dangers confronting us, so that French, as well as the three Irishmen here, know the odds at which we will fight. Loch Swilly is our landing point, but we have already been blown off course by importunate winds, and the time lost will give the British navy a chance to learn the truth of us, so much of the value of our fine espionage has been lost." He rose. "See to your arms, gentlemen, see to your men; there is no turning back now, for we are already committed. We make this landing on Irish soil or die in the attempt."

I looked around at the stern faces of those young French

officers; as long as God allows me to serve my country, the faces of these allies will stay in my mind. I heard Wolfe Tone say quietly, "That will be all, gentlemen. You may leave. But the two Irish officers will stay behind, if you please."

After the French had gone, Wolfe Tone said, "Please be seated, for there is something of importance I wish to discuss with you."

Side by side we sat to attention, and he continued, "Because you are Irish, the English will deal with you differently from the French if you are captured—you realize this?"

"If Ireland falls, sir, they can shoot us an' have done wi' it, there's no cause for complaint," said Mike.

"Ah, yes, but they may not," came the reply. "And I would be doing less than my duty if I did not warn you of a further danger. I am already guilty of treason against the English throne, and now so are you, because you are personally assisting me in an attack upon the English rule in Ireland."

"We'll take what's coming, sir," I said.

He said, smiling, "Do you realize that the punishment for treason is the barbaric business of hanging, drawing, and quartering?"

"A man can only die once, sir," remarked Mike.

"True, Hearne, but we owe to Ireland the manner of our death. Death by shooting, we accept. But it is an affront to our country's dignity that we be dragged like felons through a jeering English crowd to a public place of execution, there to be knifed and dangled on nooses. There is an escape from the humiliating touch of such captors." From his pocket he drew a little silver penknife and tossed it onto the table before us. I picked it up. Engraved upon its handle were the words: *In life, the blade that severs; in death, the blade that heals.*

Wolfe Tone said softly, "If I am taken and the death is by shooting, like a soldier, this is all right. But I will not give to Ireland's history the uncivilized death that our enemy reserves for the men she calls traitors, and neither will you. This is an order."

To my astonishment Mike said, "I've given a wee thought to it, sir. But it's tricky to know how to hide such a blade. For my part, I've got one slipped into the leather of Pepi's collar . . ."

Wolfe Tone smiled. "You're not such a fool, Hearne." He turned to me. "And you, Regan?"

These men, like my father, were Protestants. But my mother, a devout Catholic, would have told me that to take my life was a mortal sin. Now I felt unsure and confused. "I'll give some thought to it, sir," I said.

Now we rolled in a pea-green, tumultuous sea. The glass dropped lower, and the great ship ducked and floundered in the hissing troughs of a roaring gale. Soaked, disheveled, and pallid with sickness, the French soldiers staggered up onto the flowing decks, there to reel against the rails in spewing misery. The horses of the dragoons were falling in their stalls and the cannon breaking loose amidships and barging about in thunderous crashes, injuring the brave French sailors sent below to secure them. And as day after day went by, the wind rose to hurricane force, unrelenting in its purpose to drive us to the sea bed. Spars and sails were carried away, and of the remainder of the squadron there was no sign. Special flash lanterns were hung out at the mastheads by sailors with nerves of iron, but no answering lights came from the roaring wastes of the sea.

After five days of terror, the sea relented. With that dawn came a watery sun, smiling down on the battered *Hoche* in the middle of an empty ocean.

With tattered sails, splintered bulwarks, and three feet of water in the ballast holds, we rode gently before a zephyr wind on a calm, mirrored sea. For a day and a night we sailed for the northeast stars while the weakened infantry, the flower of Bonaparte's army, rested in silence on the moon-swept decks.

I was down below feeding Mia when I heard the old, familiar cry: "Land on the starboard bow!"

Mike put his head around the stall. "Did ye hear that, John. Land, land—it's old Ireland!"

Mia took a belt at me with a hind hoof, for she hated to be left in the middle of a feed, but missed, and I was up on deck like greased tallow, shoving to the rail amid a hundred excited Frenchmen. But their chattering was silenced by the next call from the crow's-nest: "Sail on the larboard bow, sir. Nay—two. Sail ahoy!"

Mike said, "With Sheep Haven and Loch Swilly on the starboard and the British squadron comin' on the larboard, God help us."

"Don't talk stupid," I replied. "England may be the queen of the sea, but it'd be more than luck if she arrived with us at the same place at the same time."

But I was uneasy within myself. There was no more cunning enemy than the British Admiralty. With men like Nelson and Borlase Warren scouring the seas, anything could happen.

"One, two, three, four, five sail on the larboard bow!" came a wail from the crow's-nest.

"The British!" said a man beside me, fear in his voice.

The Frenchmen stared about them with growing panic. The infantry swayed at the rail of the *Hoche*. Telescope glasses were appearing among the blue-clad officers of the poop and bridge. Men began to run for arms, shouting to their comrades in the bunks, for these ships were death-traps in an action. *"Les Anglais, les Anglais!"*

"Quartermaster!" cried a voice, and I recognized the commodore. "Can you identify the sail?"

"Not yet, sir!" The quartermaster on the high poop raised his glass.

"Clear decks for action, if you please."

"Clear decks—look lively, come on, *lively!*"

Dimly, on the horizon, I made out a mizzen mast and

topsail, then another. Closer, closer they came, and, when the sun slanted down through the dawn mist, the sails and masts resolved themselves into three ships. Then a yell from the crow's-nest, "Three ships only, sir—and French!"

French!

Relief swept through the waiting troops.

"Slacken mainsheets, loosen tops'ls, Bos'n. Can you clear them, Quartermaster?"

"Schooner, sir. Looks like the *Biche*, sir!"

"The *Biche!*"

We had found some of the rest of the force. The voice from the crow's-nest shouted, "Frigates *Loire* and *Résolue* two points larboard, sir!"

Rum was run out, toasts were shouted in French and English.

"Land on the starboard bow now, sir!"

Mike gripped me. "Old Ireland at last, and the British a thousand miles away! Loch Swilly!"

"Sail on the larboard bow!" The voice from the crow's-nest held a note of jubilation.

"That's the rest of the fleet," I said.

A midshipman cried, "Captain's orders, Bos'n—hard over with the helm, take her in with the wind."

"Hard over, sir!"

The big ship heeled as the helm went down, and the wind took her goosewinged and free for the bar of Loch Swilly. Slowly, the ragged rocks of Dunaff Head made shape; green began to appear on the headlands of Fanad.

Lumbering before a stiff southeasterly, as if in relief that this was the end of her journey, the *Hoche* plowed toward the entrance of the loch, and behind her, in perfect line, came the schooner and two frigates. The dragoon and infantry officers were ringing the landing bells, and French troops with muskets were running over the decks. Deck covers were flung off and block tackles lowered into the holds for the cannon and equipage; hostlers loaded with harness and saddle leather were running for the horse stalls. It was a scene of cool activity, and watching it, I felt a new, pulsating excitement. For this could be the end of Ireland's agony. A few weeks from now my country might be free. And all the blood that had been spilled, all the pain endured made worthwhile. This could be the end of the sacrifice and tears, for we would drive the hated English from the land.

"Stand by the guns! Run out larboard, Quartermaster!" It was Commodore Bompart himself, and Wolfe Tone beside him. As fierce as a hawk he looked, this Irishman who was engraving his name on the scrolls of history. The stamp of war was in his face as he stared at the green land from which he had been exiled.

"More sail on the larboard bow, sir!" came the shout from the crow's-nest.

With Mike beside me, I dashed to the rail.

"That'll be the *Sémillante* and *Immortalité!*" shouted an Irish voice.

I swung to it. "From larboard? If any more French are

coming down from Malin Head they're a compass-box off course!"

I caught a glimpse of Wolfe Tone's face and saw its apprehension. If this was the British we were caught in a trap, for the only way out of Loch Swilly would be under the gallows. He shouted aloft, "French, surely! Can't you see, man?"

"Six more sail away to larboard, sir."

Stricken, the ship's company stared. Slowly around Malin Head a string of mainmasts were appearing, first the tops, then the main booms of ships of war. And even as I stared at them a puff of smoke appeared along the gunwale of the *Résolue*, the last French frigate to enter the loch. The deck of the *Hoche* shivered beneath us to the dull boom of cannon.

"She signals, sir!" shouted the quartermaster. "The *Résolue* signals!"

"She fires!" cried Wolfe Tone. "It is the British; she is engaging!"

In the faint sunlight another string of flags crept up to the mainmast of the *Résolue*. Commodore Bompart shouted, "Signals, where the devil is the signals officer?"

"Here, sir!" A bright-eyed middy came running up.

"Read, man, *read!*"

With a telescope to his eye the boy said, " '*Résolue* to Commodore. British squadron . . . six sail of the line . . . one razee of sixty guns . . . two frigates . . . am engaging. . . .' "

"Six sail of the line!" whispered the commodore beside me. "God in Heaven . . ."

And even as he spoke little puffs of cotton wool appeared miraculously along the larboard of the two leading British ships. Light winked and flashed down the black bulwarks, and the dawn exploded in bright spitfires of flame. I stared seaward, horrified, for the *Résolue* visibly shuddered. In a vortex of flame, the mast and rigging blew up from her poop, sailing lazily down like black birds onto the sheen of the sea and spouting foam. Again the leading British fired. Off the *Résolue*'s larboard quarter a fountain of water plumed skyward; splinters shot up from her bows.

"They will blow us out of the sea," said Wolfe Tone behind me.

Bompart replied, "They have trapped us at the mouth, *mon Colonel*. Will you tell me where these British come from? One moment the sea is empty, next we have a squadron!"

Wolfe Tone replied, "They were lying in the lee of Malin Head. Obviously they were forewarned. It is the hand of fate, Bompart. We have been at sea too long: time enough for the error of the French Committee to be rectified. You know the Psalms, Commodore?" Wolfe Tone looked at the sky. " 'How long wilt Thou forget me, O Lord? How long wilt Thou hide Thy face from me?' "

"Psalm 13, *mon Colonel*," said Bompart, "but do not quote Psalms. From the time of the Spanish Armada, God has been on the side of England, and He is on their side now." He shouted, hands to his mouth, "Larboard two points, Helmsman!"

"Larboard two points, sir!"

"Load and wait, all guns starboard!"

"Load an' wait, starboard, sir!" yelled the quartermaster.

A silence came from the sea. The *Biche* was hoisting out a longboat while making full sail toward us. The *Résolue* was standing square to the English guns, her bowsprit and foresail raking the sky at a splintered angle. And the great three-riggers of Admiral Borlase Warren came on for us with full sail spread, the white foam plowing up at their blunt prows, and as they heeled past the unfortunate *Résolue* they blinded her with a tempest of grapeshot from their carronades. And though the *Loire* let fly at them with a broadside of cannon, they came on disdainfully. Now guns flashed along their tarred bulwarks, and the *Loire* reeled as twenty sixteen-pounders grooved and smashed her from bow to poop, sending her timbers shooting into the sky. The whole ocean seemed to tear asunder then as the full-throated roar of the English cannon reached us in the loch, and the screams of mutilated men sighed over the sea.

"By God, they're taking a hammering!" shouted Mike.

"It's nothing to what we'll be takin' ten minutes from now," I bellowed back. Now the *Résolue* was afire. Walls of flame welled up her midships and spilled in a scarlet mushroom over the dawn. And, even as I watched, the *Loire,* with all guns blazing, exploded to the pounding cannon of a frigate and two sails of the line. The dawn was rent with scarlet light. A towering column of water and smoke reached into the sky, and when the smoke cleared, the sea was empty. Only the bobbing foam and gently raining debris told of a ship that was no longer there. And in that interlude of silence, I heard Commodore Bompart's voice, clear and strong: "Master gunner, run out the larboard guns!"

"Run out larboard, sir!"

"Load and wait!"

"Load and wait, sir!" yelled the quartermaster.

"Bos'n, prepare to receive longboat from the *Biche!*"

"Fenders out, prepare, prepare—longboat comin', sir!"

I ran to the rail, staring down at the *Biche*'s longboat as she clamped the side of the *Hoche,* and a devil-may-care midshipman shouted up, "Captain's compliments, sir. Signals shot away, sir—do we fight it out?"

"You can do no good here, lad," cried the commodore. "Return compliments to your captain, tell him to get under way! No—wait, wait!" Bompart swung to Wolfe Tone, crying above the wind, "Take my orders to leave the ship, Colonel. We may strike our colors in the end, but we will only be prisoners of war—for you it is the gallows."

"I will take my chance with the *Hoche,* sir," replied Tone.

"But our contest is hopeless—live to fight again for Ireland, man!"

Anger filled Wolfe Tone's face. "Shall history say that I fled while the French did my fighting?"

"*Mon Colonel,* I beg of you—"

"The English are here, Commodore—tell the officer to go. Leave me to my fate, for this is how God wills it." He swung to the ship's company. "Is there any Irishman here who wants to run to France?"

There was no reply. Wolfe Tone smiled around at the intent faces of the French. "That, gentlemen, is an Irish reply. Send the schooner about her business. We fight to the death, if need be."

With their black bulwarks grinning with cannon and red signal rockets exploding in stars above them, the great English men of war bellowed down on us. Like gigantic birds of prey they came, four seventy-gun ships of the line and a frigate, the terrors of the sea, full pelt for the lonely *Hoche* with her back to Ireland.

"About she goes!" shouted Bompart. "Take them as they come, full broadsides. *Vive la France!*"

"To the death," came the answer. "*Vive la France!*"

The world seemed to erupt about us then. The deck leaped beneath me as the *Hoche* fired. Tongues of flame reached out for the oncoming English and we shipped green water as we rolled to the recoil of the broadside. Spars and timbers shot up from the English ships, and they staggered momentarily, then came on.

In the growing clamor of the battle I heard a voice, loud and clear: "For God, for honor, for Ireland!"

It was Wolfe Tone, already stripped to the waist as he manned the guns. Like a Greek god he looked, standing there with the sun of Ireland glowing on his bright hair.

The Death of a Ship

I opened my eyes to sunlight; a molten sun was directly overhead. And in the mist of slowly returning consciousness, I looked about me.

The top deck was heaped with dead. French infantry and sailors lay together in a confusion of blood, their uniforms mating in ghastly contrast in the golden sun. I did not move, believing this to be death. And then the heat of the day began to beat about me, and I rose to a sitting position, dragging myself up by gripping dangling cordage. All three masts were down, suspended in a web of sheets and canvas, and in this gossamer net were entangled the bodies of men, dead and living. There was no sound on the sea save their groans. And then I heard more sounds, and staggered upright, wiping blood from my face. The ball that had felled me must have been spent, and had clubbed me down from behind like the blow of a cudgel. I sat up, feeling my throbbing head, and remembered the searing grapeshot, the shriek of the cannister that swept our decks, and the shattering thrusts of the English six-pounders as we took broadsides at point-blank range, out-numbered five to one. The scuppers of the once-majestic *Hoche*, the pride of the French, now flowed with blood. Her shattered ribs had opened and the sea poured in, list-ing her heavily to port. Not a gun was left unsmashed, not a member of her crew uninjured. From her cockpits came the pitiful crying of men; the dead stared blankly at a brilliant Irish sun. And in that music of death I heard the sound of oars.

Staggering to the smashed rail, I stared around. Three ships of the line, a razee, and a frigate were standing to about us, their tangled rigging and torn bulwarks telling of the pugnacity of the outgunned *Hoche*. And below me was an English gig being rowed by bonneted sailors. In the stern, bowed under in their defeat, sat Commodore Bompart and his captured officers. Among the officers, I instantly recognized Wolfe Tone.

A low cry came from an upturned twenty-pounder be-side me, and I turned.

"Mike," I said.

He was lying where the snout of the cannon had pinned him, and blood was on his face. I tore at the tangled skein of ropes and iron that held him, and he groaned as the cannon rolled an inch, pinning him.

"Don't bother yourself," he said. "Can't ye see I'm finished, man?"

I bowed my head.

"Och, for heaven's sake," said he. "Weeping, is it, when the fair country's slippin' from under your feet!"

I did not turn to him, and he said, "Should ye be loungin' round here, Regan, when the big fella's in the hands o' the English?"

"I—I am away to him now," I said.

"Then you'd better take this, for he might be needin' it." He raised his free hand and I took from his fingers a little shining thing.

"It's Wolfe Tone's little knife—d'ye remember it?" His voice sank to a whisper and he stiffened to the pain. "They —they took his arms from him, you see, and I found this on the deck." He grinned at me. "Were they thinkin' maybe he'd be holing the English fleet wi' it, eh?"

The sun burned down. Faintly came the lapping of the sea and the creak of outraged iron; the wounded whimpered from the smashed cockpits.

"Will ye do a thing for me, John Regan?"

I gripped his hand. "Aye, man, aye."

"I've no people, see, so nobody much'll miss me. Just wee Pepi down in the bunks with me hammock. Will ye see to Pepi?"

"I will that."

He sighed, and there spread over his face a timeless joy, and he smiled. "Just wee Pepi and the beloved land." He closed his eyes, whispering, "Even from here I can smell the September sweetness of her. Can ye see her from here, Regan?"

I raised my face and saw the rolling green of Ireland blazing in the noonday sun. "Aye," I said.

The shimmering estuary rippled like quicksilver, and the

peaks of the Sperrin Mountains trumpeted against the flashing blue of the sky.

"She's beautiful indeed this morning," I said. "Can ye smell the fields, Mike, for the folk of Buncrana are out wi' the harvest!"

But he did not answer. Quite still he lay, and his hand, outstretched on the bloodstained deck, was pointing to Ireland.

"Good-by, man," I said and rose.

The knife of Wolfe Tone was hot in my clenched fingers.

Now the ship lurched beneath me, and fear struck me afresh as I clambered over the shambles of the deck and groped a path down the companionway ladders to the officers' bunks. Here the sea was washing and thundering to each new roll of the dying *Hoche*, but I found Pepi easily, sitting in Mike's hammock. She licked my face as I snatched her against me. His flute was beside her, and I took this, too, and also his beggar's bundle, since I might need this disguise to make an escape from Loch Swilly. In the uniform of the United Irishmen I wouldn't get a mile, this I knew. The *Hoche* was bellowing now as the sea took her, and with Pepi in my arms, I staggered through the heaving corridors and down a ladder to the bottom deck.

But I never reached the bottom deck, for the hull was flooded.

Standing on the ladder, waist deep in creeping water, I shouted, "Mia, Mia, *Mia!*"

There was no answer but the pitiless wallow of the incoming sea.

Clinging to the ladder in that place where two hundred horses drowned, I wept for my second friend to die that day. In great shuddering sobs, I wept for Mia.

But the dead, men and horses, have dried their tears, my father once said to me—do not weep for them, weep for the living.

And so, with the living Wolfe Tone in my mind, I changed swiftly from the uniform of the United Irishmen into the beggar's rags of Mike Hearne. On the larboard side, hidden from the English men of war, I dropped a rope down into the sea and, with Pepi in my arms, let myself down it.

"Keep your head up, woman," I said. It was dusk by the time we reached the shore.

In a wayside quarry clear of the beach I wrung out my soaked clothing and then shivered back into them, for the night was coming October-cold and I was chattering to freeze.

Next I took Pepi into my arms and explained how her master was dead and that I was her master now, and though she could not weep, her eyes went big at me under the rise of the moon. Then I took off her collar and felt for the knife that Mike said was there, but I did not find it. I realized then that Mike must have extracted it during the attack when all seemed hopeless. So I put in its place the tiny silver penknife that belonged to my hero, Wolfe Tone.

Then the beggar and his dancing dog took the road to Letterkenny. And although he couldn't flute in tune, this beggar played to keep his spirits up, with Pepi dancing down the winding road before him under the light of the October moon.

The rebellion was crushed in Ireland. Our last hope had been captured by the enemy and soon would die. So there remained to this beggar one last and vital duty—to give his master the freedom to die as he wished and to cheat his captors of their last revenge on his beloved Ireland.

The English Trader

Because Wolfe Tone's escort was horsed, it had the legs of me. But by running and walking and by traveling by night when they were sleeping, I overtook them at Strabane and waited on a bright October morning for the dragoons to bring their prisoner through.

The patriot Irish were weeping in Strabane that morning, and the memory of that scene is branded in my mind; I see it still.

With a great flourishing of scarlet tunics and clanking brass the escort came, and there were enough of them to guard a hundred prisoners. Fifty strong they were, mounted on their great white stallions, with streamer pennants tickling the wind and their great silver sabers tenting their surcoats behind them. Bareheaded was Wolfe Tone, with his tunic torn, and the mare that carried him was near bony to her grave. But he sat her like some ancient prince, his hair bright in the autumn sunlight, his head erect and proud despite the indignity of his fettered hands. And thus did they parade this Irish patriot—from Ramelton through Omagh and Dungannon to Drogheda and the barracks of Dublin. And the patriot Irish, at the risk of the whip, came out of their cabins and stood in deep throngs by the roadside as he passed, and many knelt in the gutter in prayer for him and others wept.

I too wept for my country as Wolfe Tone passed by, and from the pavement crowds I raised Pepi high, that he could see her and know he was not forgotten. For a moment only Tone turned his eyes to me, and I saw in them his recognition, despite my disguise. Nodding, he gazed past me. Had he put his hand in mine and blessed me, I could have known no greater reward.

"Come on, girl, to hell out o' here," I said to Pepi. "We're bound for Dublin city and the English Trader and Derry O'Shea, the fighting Irishman."

For over the length and breadth of the land of the shamrock, come defeat and indignity, the whip or the pillory, there'll always be Irishmen to fight for the land at the drop of a hat. And we in the movement knew them all. This one was the escape expert Caine Adams had told me of, the man who had saved more United Irishmen from the English gallows than had half the Irish rebel army.

The English Trader, the inn outside Dublin barracks— a queer old name, come to think of it. Here was a recovery post run by an Irish patriot in the very teeth of the English army. *Derry O'Shea:* the name beat in my head.

So we danced at every inn on the road between Strabane and Dublin, Pepi and I, and though I was no great

shakes on the whistle, Pepi made up for it with her dancing. By day we traveled now, by night we played in the
taprooms in a whirl of bright colors, with the turncoat
militia kicking up their spurs with the prancing maidens,
and the ale flowing out under the doors. And after the last
drunk had been eased out with a chair leg, we would creep
into the stables and bury ourselves in the hay, and Pepi's
little sleek body was warm under my hand. But although
she danced like a dog delighted, I reckon she was dying
inside like me, for she would cry in her sleep and then
wake up licking me, only to cry again because I wasn't
Mike Hearne. In this manner, dancing and crying, we
reached the city of Dublin and the inn called the English
Trader.

It was a tumbledown old ramshackle if ever I saw one,
right outside the gate of the barracks of Dublin, so the
landlord could see the comings and goings.

But if this particular landlord was the fighting Irishman
called Derry O'Shea, I'd have another think coming. He
was an ale-soaked, blue-nosed wreck of an old man and a
toady to the English redcoats, with his Good day to ye,
fine sir, and welcome you are, soldier, providing you're
wearin' the blood-red coat of England and not the Irish
green.

"And what's wrong with the Irish green, landlord?"
asked a young English sergeant, handsome in his red and
gold.

"Well, yer honor," wheezed the landlord, "I've no time

for the fellas meself—though, true, I earn me livin' among them, but ye canna trust an Irishman, ye know—dacent or indacent!"

"Why not?" came the reply. "I've met some fine ones." The young soldier jerked his thumb at the barracks behind him. "There's an Irishman in there this moment I'd trust with my life, though I shouldn't be saying it. And when he goes to the rope—which he will—the world will be short of another six-foot man."

I sat in the corner, face lowered, with the flute in one hand and Pepi in my lap.

The landlord cried, pouring the sergeant's ale, "Is that the fella they call Wolfe Tone who tried to bring the Frenchies in up on Loch Swilly?"

"If you were a real Irishman yourself, you'd know," said the sergeant. "What's wrong with you people?"

"Och, don't take me for an Irishman, Sergeant, sir. Dear God, I was born within sight of the Dublin spires, 'tis true, but I'm English in me heart after serving the porter to you fine English gentlemen!"

Distaste filled the sergeant's face. He sank his quart pewter and barged through the inn door.

I said from my corner, "Is this inn called the English Trader, landlord?"

"That's what the sign says, beggar, and why might ye be asking?" His little red-rimmed eyes peered at me from the untidy folds of his face.

"Then can ye tell me where I can find a decent Irishman, not a wheedling wreck like you?"

"Has this fella a name, then?" asked he, unabashed.

"Derry O'Shea."

Lifting a quart, he said, "Och, that fella? He was doin' a fine, fierce job from the taproom here—hooking the Irish prisoners out o' the cells under the noses of the English, and they came and fetched him for it, an' he never came back, poor soul."

"God help him," I whispered, putting down my glass. "I came to find a patriot, and all I found was you."

With Pepi clutched against me I went to the door and swung it wide.

"Are the streets empty, beggar?" asked the landlord behind me, and I turned back to him.

He said, "Because, providing they are, I'd be willing to discuss this fella Derry O'Shea a mite further." Now that we were alone in the taproom, he put his finger in his ale and traced a shamrock on the counter before him and began to whistle a quaint old Irish air.

Said he, "He left under guard, d'ye see, son. And he's never been heard of since. But there's always good men ready to step into the shoes of a patriot man. Me name is Patsy Hannigan, and Derry was me friend before he died. Will this suffice ye?"

I shut the door, approaching him. "You have taken his place?"

"I have. And I'm in the same business. Now, don't ye think that's clever, youngster? Would any living creature suspect I'd be fool enough to take over from Derry O'Shea and continue his business under the noses of the English?"

"You're either a brave man or a traitor," I replied. "How do you expect me to trust you?"

He shrugged. "Ye can't, son. But who can trust who these days? For instance, if I were to tell you I was after saving the life of the greatest o' them all, Wolfe Tone, you'd likely skate to the Provost Prison and inform on me and have me arrested."

I peered into the sodden face, and he said huskily, "Don't look too hard, lad. It's a face that plays its part, and I got it like that in service to the country." He added, "My life's near an end, so come quick with it—what d'ye want of me, old Patsy Hannigan?"

"Help—for the master," I replied.

"God bless you," he wheezed. "Do ye realize he's in the Provost Prison and that has four walls? And in those four walls there is a cell, and he's inside that? And the gaol itself lies within the four walls of the barracks of Dublin?"

"Walls have doors," I whispered.

"He's the kernel of the nut, son. Ye'll never extract him without crackin' the shell, and ye'll need a thousand infantry wi' cannon to do that!" He turned away in despair. "You're young, son, and you're fiery. But it'll take more than enthusiasm to lift Wolfe Tone out o' the barracks of Dublin, unless you hire Napoleon." Deep he drank, eyes closed, and wiped his sweating face with the back of his hand. "Dear God, I've been sittin' here wonderin' and schemin'."

I said, glancing around the empty taproom, "I've got to trust you, Hannigan. I've got no option." I stooped, hook-

ing Pepi up onto the bar counter. From her collar I took
Wolfe Tone's tiny knife. "There's no hope of getting him
out," I said, "so I'm going to try to get this in."

"Is that all Ireland asks of us, then?" His eyes opened
wide in wonder.

"It is all he is asking," I replied. "There is nothing more
we can do. If the sentence is hanging, drawing, and quartering, he has got to have this knife."

"Ye can take it as a foregone conclusion," said he, "that
never in this life will they give him death by shooting.
You're aimin' to take it in there, then?"

"If it can be done."

He pondered this. "You might get over the main wall
into the barracks all right, son, but there's another wall
round the yard of the Provost Prison."

"No odds to that," I answered. "How high is it?"

"About eight feet. A sprightly lad like you might scale
it at the time the master takes his exercise."

"They allow prisoners out for exercise?"

"Och, for sure—ye can hear them clanging that cell
door every morning at six and they put them under lock
and key again before dusk, for safety's sake."

"Then I'll try it."

"You can try it, lad, but you'll not get away with it.
You've got to reach the man, remember, to hand him the
knife, and the guard would shoot you down like a dog
before you got within feet of him. You'd never get out
alive."

"Talking of dogs," I said, "Pepi might do it."

"What nonsense are ye speaking?"

I said, drawing closer, "Listen, Pepi *could* do it. The master knows she's carrying a knife. He knows her and she knows him. If we could get her into his exercise yard she'd go straight up to him."

He scratched his ear reflectively. "Nobody would shoot a dog," said he. "Least of all this wee thing. And come to think of it, the barracks is running with 'em—every color, shape, and size."

"I could put her over the wall . . ."

"Not good enough. That would only land her in the barracks area." He frowned at the ceiling. "But if you climbed the main wall with her and got onto the square, you might be able to pull yourself up on top of the inner wall around the exercise yard."

"And lower Pepi down inside?"

"That's it," Hannigan replied.

"Just before the master is let out for his exercise."

"Aye, but you'd have to watch that, for he'd have an escort with him—a sergeant, more than likely, so he'd be no fool."

"You mean he'd shoot Pepi?"

"Och, no—he'd not do that. He'd think she came under the gate, but he'd likely shoot you if he saw ye on the wall."

"So it could be done," I whispered.

"If you can get into the barracks and then on top of the wall around Provost Prison, you can get the dog to

Wolfe Tone's feet, practically, but I don't give ye much chance of coming out of it alive."

He poured himself a tot of whiskey and drank it at a swallow. "Queer thing, you come to think of it, about soldiers." His eyes narrowed in the light of the lamp. "They can hang, draw, and quarter a man, but they wouldn't lift a boot against a dog." He slapped down the glass. "If you can get Pepi into that exercise yard, you'll be home and dry."

Anxiously I asked, "When does the trial start?"

"It's a court-martial, for Tone's a soldier. It started the day before yesterday—I saw General Loftus come in with Major Armstrong in the morning. And the judge advocate was there an hour after."

"Might he get a fair trial?"

"Aye, the trial will be fair enough, but he's convicted already. There's no hope for an Irishman who bears arms against the King."

"When will we know the sentence?"

He shrugged. "This time tomorrow, more than likely."

"Then if it's a hanging judge, I'll go in tomorrow night. Can you give me a map of the prison?"

He sighed. "For sure, it'll be two Irishmen hanging."

"My business. You just give me a map of the prison."

A strange thing happened then. He clasped his hands and raised his eyes upward, saying, "Oh, God, grant me the courage of Derry O'Shea! Grant me the sinews to go in there with him . . ."

"You're more use here, Patsy Hannigan," I said.

"It's a perilous state we're in indeed, youngster, that the fate of Ireland's hero should rest in the hands of a boy with a dog."

"Give me that map," I repeated, "and leave the rest to me."

He nodded, pulling out a pencil stub and a scrap of paper. He said, drawing clumsily, "At eight o'clock tomorrow night, then?"

"Aye. Mark the spots where I can get over the wall."

He replied, "It'll not go easy for you if they catch ye, you realize that? Think yourself lucky if it's only transportation for life."

I said softly, "Patsy Hannigan"—he raised his weary, lined face to mine—"if you inform on me, I'll kill you in the name of Ireland. If they transport me, I'll escape and find you. If they hang me, I'll haunt ye—d'ye hear me? If they leave me with a soul, it will never let you rest."

He smiled at me. "This is where you get over the main wall," he said. "Once inside the barracks, you'll see the wall of the exercise yard away to the right. On the other side of that wall you'll find Wolfe Tone. May God grant me the strength to be of further use to you. Now, away upstairs to the room above this, for the soldiers are coming."

With Pepi held against me I went quickly up the creaking stairs. I did not dare to light the lamp by the narrow bed but held up the map to the light of the moon.

The Healing Blade

At dusk the next evening they began to build the gallows.

I sat on the edge of the bed in the English Trader and listened to the hammering of the carpenters and their shouts of gruff laughter, and there was within me a sickness I could not quell. From below came the bass voices of men and the stamping of dragoon horses tethered outside on the cobbles. I looked out of the tiny leaded window and saw, through the gathering darkness, a solitary yellow light glowing from the barracks that held Wolfe Tone, the last hope of Irish freedom. The barracks wall was black and grisly against the beam.

All around me the small lights of my life had gone out one by one. First my father had gone, shot down in an ambush on the road to Fishguard, then Caine Adams. Mike Hearne and Patrick Hays, my new friend and my old one, had also died in the cause of Ireland. And my beloved Mia, who did not know why she died, caught by the flood in the horse stalls of the doomed *Hoche*.

And now this man, the one in the world most precious

to my country, might die the degrading death all patriots feared.

With Pepi held against me, I shivered at the window, for I still did not trust Patsy Hannigan. Men were abroad these days who would sell a man for the price of his shirt, and this rusted, ale-soaked wreck was no Derry O'Shea, the fighting Irishman of whom Caine Adams had spoken. For myself I was not afraid now; even the terror of the Spanish galleys no longer assailed me. But it was necessary for me to live so that Wolfe Tone might save Ireland's dignity in the manner of his dying.

I swung to face the door of the tiny room as footsteps thumped on the stairs.

The door came open. Panting, disheveled, Hannigan stood there in the dusk.

"Are ye ready, son?"

"What—what about the customers?"

"I've hied the soldiers out o' the taproom, saying the barrels are dry. The dray comes again within the hour, so it's now or never."

"You've heard the sentence?"

"I've heard the talk of it from the troops: the music of the gallows is proof enough, and our own common sense. You have the wee dog?" He peered.

"Aye, here."

"And the knife's in place?"

"Safer than death," I said. "And it may be death for one of us to see it's delivered to Tone—d'ye realize this?"

"Your death, not mine, young 'un. I'm taking ye to the wall, but it's your job to go over it." He smiled at me, and I thought, Yes, and the moment I'm over it you'll go hell for leather to the gate and ring out the guard, and they'll blow Pepi's legs from under her before she gets a yard, but I said, "Let's have no more hot air about it, then—take me to the place."

His eyes drifted over me in quiet amusement. "How old are you, son?"

"Nigh eighteen, but it's not important."

"Any age is important when it comes to death. If they put ye to the rope with Tone a week from now ye'll not have begun to live."

"Take me to the wall," I said.

We left the English Trader by the back. It was still light in the streets, and the rope I carried was secure on my shoulder and Pepi was snug under my arm. The little iron hook caught on the first throw, and I pulled myself up from Hannigan's back, hand over hand, and peered over the barracks wall. Swords of light thrust across the deserted square.

"Are ye all right, then?" Hannigan's face peered up at me from the ground.

I nodded. With a thumping heart I put Pepi on top of the wall, dropped the rope over the other side, and went down to the square with her licking the back of my hand, enjoying every minute. She whined then, in question.

"Hush, you!" I whispered, and gripping her, dropped to the ground.

Crouched there in shadow, I listened. Nothing moved within the great stone walls. Distantly a clock struck the hour of eight. I heard a door open and slam, the commanding voices of the guard, and the unmistakable clatter of armed men. Running swiftly across the cobbles I gained the shorter wall that surrounded Provost Prison, and knelt in a pier abutment, listening. All was silent at first, and then I heard tramping footsteps. They appeared to be receding. I tried a jump to get a hand on top of the wall, but it was too high, so I coiled my rope and little grapnel for the fling, then drew it back with a start. For now the footsteps were directly behind the wall where I was crouching. Praying, I waited. The sounds died away: silence. And then, to my joy, I heard Wolfe Tone's voice, but faintly, as if he and his escort had strolled to the other side of the yard. Quickly, I threw the grapnel. It missed the first time but caught on the second, and I drew the rope taut. Sweat ran in little streams down my face as I lay against the wall, listening. I climbed, panting, with Pepi clinging on for dear life and wondering what in Hades was happening.

Slowly, with infinite care, I raised my eyes over the wall of the Provost Prison.

Wolfe Tone and the sergeant of the guard were standing not fifty feet away, talking earnestly together. Beyond them the door of the cell block was open. With the utmost care, nerves tingling, I spread-eagled myself over the wall, one hand gripping the parapet, the other hand holding Pepi. Reaching down, I dropped her the last four feet onto the flagstones. She landed easily and rolled to square herself, staring up at me in blank astonishment in the moment before I loosened the grapnel and dropped out of her sight back into the barracks compound. There I crouched, hardly daring to breathe.

Not a sound then but wind-whisper up and down the wall and Pepi crying to me, wondering where I had gone. Then I heard the sergeant's voice, and I recognized it instantly as the man I had seen drinking in the English Trader, and I cursed my luck for he had seen Pepi before.

"The barracks is full of dogs and cats," said he, striding over. "Where did this one come from?"

"Under the gate, more than likely, Sergeant," replied Wolfe Tone.

"Was it here when we came into the yard, for I didn't see it."

"She's an attractive wee dog, is she not?"

My heart nearly stopped beating when the sergeant said, gruffly, "She don't look like a barracks scavenger to me, and I could swear I've seen her before. Better put her down, sir."

"Would you deny me a minute with a friendly little dog, Sergeant?"

"By the fuss she's making of you, you might be a long-lost friend."

Then I heard Wolfe Tone say, "Thank you, little dog, for bringing me new hope. Now away, back to your master," and I knew he spoke to me.

It was all that was necessary. I put my face against the cold stone and gave a prayer of thanks.

I was turning away for the run across the square to the barracks wall when the redcoat soldier came.

He was away to the town, being off duty, I think. He looked imposing in his tunic of scarlet and gold and his tight blue trews, and he peered at me in the semi-darkness, some quaint trick of the rising moon making him gigantic against the stars. And as he opened his mouth for the cry, I leaped. With a strength born of desperation, I launched myself at him, catching him a glancing blow with my right. As he staggered back, astonishment on his face, I caught him again and he flattened against the wall. I gripped his tunic, arm drawn back, but his eyes were closed. Pressing my body against him, I slid him down to the ground. I listened. There was no sound but the wind.

Snatching up the rope, I ran across the square, ducking along the pilasters and piers of the wall. Here, panting, I swung up the grapnel, but it did not catch. Instead, jagged pieces of glass tumbled in little crashes onto the cobblestones. Lights began to shaft the square as barrack doors came open. A man shouted, then another. Gritting my teeth, I again swung the little hook over the wall, and again it slid down free in a crash of glass. Coiling the rope,

I ran along the wall again, seeking a place where the grapnel would hold, and paused to swing it up. I saw it momentarily suspended against the faint stars, and then it slithered down the wall again, belling and clanging amid the stones at my feet.

Now I raced along, careless of noise, dragging the grapnel after me, repeatedly skidding to a stop to swing it over the wall, but never did it even begin to hold. Men were running now, their hobnailed boots thumping about in the darkness; commands were roared. And as I dropped the grapnel and made a desperate run for the barracks gate in a last bid for life, I heard a voice cry, "Put that gun down, Hannigan, have ye gone raving?"

"It's the landlord of the Trader, sir—he's covering the sentry."

And then Patsy Hannigan shouted, "Take the barracks gate, son—come through the main gate!"

Thudding footsteps behind me now. The gate loomed up fifty yards ahead.

"Come on, lad, *come on!*"

"I'm telling you for the last time, Hannigan!"

"Run, *run!*"

It was Patsy Hannigan seeking his manhood in the memory of Derry O'Shea. He cried, "Take another step, sir—just take another, an' I'll blast ye to kingdom come. Regan, where the devil have ye got to, come on, come on!"

And then, loud and clear above the disorganized shouts

and military commands, a man's voice wailed from Provost Prison: "A surgeon, in the name of Heaven! Will somebody fetch a surgeon! It's the Irish colonel—it's Wolfe Tone!"

A shaft of light exploded at the barracks gate and I swung to it, seeing, in the instant before the red blaze died, the body of Patsy Hannigan sinking to the ground.

"In the name of God, man," shouted a voice, "did you have to shoot him in the back?"

Panting, I lay back against the wall.

I knew in my heart that the last gate had been slammed, that there was no escape, although Patsy Hannigan, a new Irish martyr, had given his life for me. But now I was beyond caring. For I was looking toward the gate of Provost Prison. Under the beam of yellow light from the cell window, I could see it clearly. A great commotion was rising there, with officers running and issuing crisp commands.

"Fetch Major Sandys at once! At once, do you hear me?"

"Is the surgeon coming, Sergeant?"

"He'll be here this minute, sir—a messenger's gone to his room."

I heard somebody say, "This will be a pretty one to answer—have you any idea how he got the knife?"

They were coming for me from the barracks gate. In single file along the wall they were coming, with the measured tread of trained soldiers. Now that the initial shock was over, discipline had returned, and they came without commotion or uttered word. But I did not care. Leaning there against the barracks wall I looked up and saw the stars, and there was in them a sudden radiant brightness.

And I felt the satisfaction of a duty attempted and done. I saw my father again, great in strength and purpose, and he was smiling. I saw him in his youth, galloping the lanes of Ireland; I was with him in the fighting with the blades of Chantilly and knelt with him in prayer for my mother at the little wayside Madonnas. I remembered, too, the portrait of my mother's face, she who had died that I might live. But, best of all, I remembered my beloved country. If they carried me across the sea to a foreign gaol, I would still dream of her. I would see again the balm of her green summers, the gold of her autumns, the hoarfrost sparkle of her beauty in winter. If my life was spared, I would take to the pen in this foreign prison, this Botany Bay where England sent her enemies. By the pen I would tell of my country and how she fought to live. I would tell of the women who gave her life, the men who schemed for her, and the patriots who died for her that she might never die.

The soldiers were closer; I heard their boots tramping on the gravel.

"Here he is!"

"Stand back, you fool, he's armed!"

They reached for me apprehensively, hands groping in the darkness.

"Och, he's only a lad, Sergeant!"

"You watch him—he laid Private Smith out cold."

The sergeant said, gripping me, "You'll get ten years for this, son—or I'm a Dutchman."

They did not beat me down as I had expected. Indeed, they were strangely kind.

Another muttered, "Being found in a British barracks after dark is transportation for sure, son, do you realize that?"

As they led me away I heard a low whining on the road. Pepi had found me and was dancing along at my feet.

"Is that your dog?" asked somebody.

"Aye."

"Kick her out of it, Joe."

I said, "Can—can I have her for a bit?"

It stopped them in their tracks. The sergeant said gruffly, "Must be off your head, bringing a dog in with you." Bending, he lifted Pepi and pushed her against me.

Beside the gates, Patsy Hannigan was lying face down on the cobbles. An officer standing over him turned at our approach and strolled arrogantly toward me.

"You were with this man?"

"Yes."

"What is your name?"

"Mick Tooley," I replied.

"You were trying to help Wolfe Tone, your officer, to escape?"

"We were."

"Well, you didn't manage it, did you!"

He was pink-faced and fresh, straight from England by his looks, and no older than I. Suddenly he smiled, and he had the face of a grown man in that strange light. He said, "But it was a good try, Irishman, for all that. You deserved to get away with it. Though even while you were trying to save him, your hero was making an attempt on his life." He added, "He may still live, but it is doubtful."

I did not reply.

"Does this surprise you?" he asked.

"A man has a right to choose his own fate," I said.

He nodded. "Perhaps," he said and came closer. "Is that your dog?"

"Yes."

"She followed you in here?"

"Yes."

"You'll have no need of her now, of course."

His eyes drifted over Pepi in quiet assessment, and I realized, with a sudden joy, that he was young enough to have an eye for a dog.

"We'd best get going, sir," said the sergeant.

"You'll get going when I tell you," came the young officer's reply.

"She—she's a dancing dog, sir," I said urgently.

He smiled. "A dancing dog! I—I have a little sister—Look, you have no need of her. If she really dances, I would like to have her . . ."

"If you feed her proper, sir," I said.

"Of course. My sister will see to that." He took Pepi

from my hands. The sergeant barked a command, and we marched off, and he muttered as we went, "Now that we've gotten rid of the dog we'll get rid of you. Get moving, son—they've no pets in Botany Bay."

The stars were brightening above me as they took me away.

Is my country dead? I wondered as they took me to the cell. Soon I might die, but I would not think of this. I would think of life, that I might serve my motherland. I would pray for her freedom, that I might see her unfettered. And I would record for unborn generations the truth of Ireland's story. Of the great Lord Edward Fitzgerald I would write, of the heroic Matthew Keugh and Bagenal Harvey—the great men of my time, patriots all! Of Father John Murphy, the beloved priest, I would tell, and of John Colclough, who had died with a smile while still young.

The cell door clanged behind me.

Alone, I listened to the tramping boots of my captors.

Rising to my feet, I faced the tiny window that looked up at the heavens, and the October night was a glory of stars. I heard the plaintive fiddles of the street beggars and the rumble of the Dublin streets. And I think I knew, standing there, that this was the end of the whip and the pillory; that a new Ireland would rise from the ashes of the old—an Ireland green and bright, a land unshackled, untorn by strife and dissent, a country reborn and free.

Free, *free!*

The answer to my prayer came to me, sweeping over me in waves of faith. Trembling, I gripped the bars of the prison window and stared at the eastern sky.

"Lady of Chantilly," I said, "grant this to me."

Historical Characters in
The Healing Blade

LORD EDWARD FITZGERALD Younger brother of the Duke of Leinster. Once a member of the Irish Parliament, he served in the American Revolution and was later dismissed from the British Army because of his radical views. Distinguished for his fine character and extreme good looks and for his courage as a soldier, Lord Edward became one of the early leaders of the United Irishmen, a society pledged to free Ireland from British rule. This secret society was formed in Belfast in 1791 by a young lawyer, Theobald Wolfe Tone, and his friend Samuel Neilson.

While Wolfe Tone was trying to raise another French expedition to support an Irish rebellion against the British, the 1798 rebellion broke out, and it was organized and led by Lord Edward. However, the British government, with spies everywhere, knew in advance of the rebels' plans, and struck first. Most of the leaders of the United Irishmen in Ireland were arrested, and among the first to be captured was Lord Edward. He fought bitterly to resist arrest, was mortally wounded, and died some three weeks later. His courage and devotion to his country were above suspicion, his ideals lofty and unselfish. He died for what he considered a sacred cause.

BAGENAL HARVEY A Protestant landowner and a man of humane and kindly disposition. Bagenal Harvey was the owner of Bargy Castle at the time of the 1798 rebellion. Though possessed of great personal courage (he fought several duels), he was not a born leader, and it is thought that he took the leadership because of popular clamor rather than for any personal ambitions. He led the rebels in a violent attack on the town of New Ross on June 5, 1798, and at first it appeared certain that they were victorious. But General Johnson, the loyalist commander, counterattacked while the rebels were celebrating and drove them from the town. When the rebellion was eventually crushed, Bagenal Harvey, who for so long had striven for moderation and had done all in his power to prevent unnecessary bloodshed, was hanged with other conspirators on the old Wexford Bridge.

CAPTAIN MATTHEW KEUGH Rebel governor of Wexford at the time of Bagenal Harvey's leadership and a man of great size, good looks, and magnetic personality. Keugh did much to prevent rebel excesses and was spoken for by the influential Lord Kingsborough, commander of the infamous North Cork Militia. Like the other rebels, he too was hanged on Wexford Bridge at the command of

General Lake, the British General Officer commanding. It is said that even in death his good looks did not desert him: that in the horrible exhibition of speared heads, his face maintained the same beauty and quiet resolution that had dignified it in life.

GENERAL GERARD LAKE   The General Officer commanding the British and Irish loyalist forces at the time of the 1798 rebellion. A born soldier, he was inflexible in purpose and merciless in victory. The sixty-five prominent persons hanged on Wexford Bridge were but a small proportion of the vast numbers who died at his command in revenge for the rebellion. Even persons found unarmed in their own houses were slain in cold blood. It is said that after he left Ireland the women and children fled from the sight of a British uniform as from an evil spirit.

FATHER JOHN MURPHY   This Catholic priest raised the first standard of revolution at Boolavogue, a hamlet on the road between Wexford and Gorey, on May 26, 1798. A statue to Father John can be seen today in the square of Enniscorthy. He is described by one set of historians as ignorant—a narrow-minded fanatic; by others he is depicted as a simple-minded son of the priesthood who was driven to desperation by the burning of his house and chapel by yeomen cavalry. His followers believed he was possessed of supernatural powers, that he could catch bullets with his fingers.

He rapidly took Oulart, Camolin, and Ferns with a

half-starved rebel army armed mainly with pikes. Following these successes he captured Enniscorthy after a big battle and camped on Vinegar Hill above the town. On May 30, driving all before him, he took Wexford itself. But the loyalists who supported the British Crown began to organize, and British troops were shipped into Ireland in vast numbers. After further successes came defeat. Father John, with hundreds of others, many of them priests, was executed. His death broke the myth of his believed invincibility.

Robespierre Leader of the Reign of Terror in the French Revolution; a man responsible for hunting down the aristocrats of France and sending them to the guillotine in groups. Later, he was executed himself.

James Napper Tandy An Irish leader who boasted that some 30,000 Irish peasants would rise to the flag of liberation and follow him if the French Directory under Napoleon Bonaparte would support such an Irish landing with French troops. Over twenty United Irishmen sailed with Napper Tandy in a fast sailing boat immediately preceding Wolfe Tone's major force. They landed on the Isle of Rathlin on September 16, 1798, and were routed at once on the Irish coast. Managing to spread a few proclamations, they then escaped to Norway. Tandy's assertions that only a small French force was necessary for the liberation of Ireland had puzzled the French Directory, since Wolfe Tone had long been insisting that a minimum of 10,000 French troops would be required at the beginning of such a conquest.

THEOBALD WOLFE TONE   One of the greatest names of Irish history, Theobald Wolfe Tone, a United Irishman, was in France serving under Napoleon in the French army when the 1798 rebellion broke out under Lord Edward Fitzgerald. Earlier, in 1796, Tone managed to persuade the French Directory in Paris to send an invasion fleet to Ireland to support a previous rebellion. On December 15, 1796, this fleet set sail from Brest with 15,000 men, seventeen large warships, and thirteen frigates. Had this great fleet landed in Ireland, it undoubtedly would have changed the course of Irish history, for the peasants were seething under the cruelty of English rule. However, tempestuous weather was encountered and, broken and battered, the invaders struggled back to Brest.

This was a serious setback in Wolfe Tone's plans. But in August 1798, as a result of his further endeavours, Napoleon sent another invasion force to Ireland under General Humbert. It was a small force but it managed to land immediately and defeated a British force twice its size. But the rebellion under Lord Edward Fitzgerald was now broken and ended, Ireland was full of British troops, and the French general soon had to surrender. Wolfe Tone persuaded yet another force of Frenchmen to attempt an invasion of Ireland two months later, and sailed with this fleet himself. But the French were attacked by a British squadron and were defeated. Tone was taken prisoner, conveyed to Dublin, and there tried and sentenced to be hanged. He asked for a soldier's death by shooting; this was refused and in October 1798, he committed suicide with a tiny knife he had managed to obtain.

ADMIRAL JOHN BORLASE WARREN The British admiral who destroyed the French fleet which attempted to land an invasion force at Loch Swilly in October 1798.

The French Revolution and the 1798 Irish rebellion had common aims. Whereas the former was a revolution against the cruelty and oppression of the aristocracy, the latter was an attempt by Ireland to throw off the yoke and tyranny of British rule which was supporting a system which enriched the landlords and impoverished the peasants.

ABOUT THE AUTHOR

ALEXANDER CORDELL is a well-known author of adult historical novels. A British subject born in Ceylon, he was educated in China and has traveled widely with the British Civil Service. He now lives in Monmouthshire, on the border of Wales, and devotes his full time to writing.

The Healing Blade is the final book in his trilogy about the Irish rebellion of 1798, which began with *The White Cockade* and *Witches' Sabbath*.